No Place for Magic

for

Magic

Tales of the Frog Princess

Tales of the Frog Princess
The story so far . . .

The Frog Princess
Dragon's Breath
Once Upon a Curse

No Place for Magic

for

Magic

Tales of the Frog Princess

E.D. BAKER

BLOOMSBURY
CHILDREN'S
BOOKS

First published in Great Britain in 2008 by Bloomsbury Publishing Plc
36 Soho Square, London, W1D 3QY

A CIP catalogue record of this book is available
from the British Library

ISBN 978 0 7475 8740 8

All papers used by Bloomsbury Publishing are natural,
recyclable products made from wood grown in well-managed
forests. The manufacturing processes conform to the
environmental regulations of the country of origin.

Printed in Great Britain by Clays Ltd, St Ives Plc

1 3 5 7 9 10 8 6 4 2

www.bloomsbury.com

This book is dedicated to Ellie for being my sounding board, to Kimmy for laughing at all the right places, to Victoria for her insight, to Nate and Emiko for their support and enthusiasm, and to all my wonderful fans who wrote to me wanting to know what happens next.

One

A tendril brushed my face, tickling me on the nose. I jerked my head back and whacked it on the table leg behind me. "Wretched plant!" I said, rubbing my head with one hand as I pushed the vine away with the other.

Ever since my aunt had returned to her normal self, she hadn't been able to keep her mind on anything but her beloved Haywood. Her magic had suffered for it, becoming muddled and not quite as she'd intended. The flowering vines she'd planted in the Great Hall to celebrate their reunion had spread across the walls, engulfed the table legs, and threatened to cover the doors and windows. Because they were too tough for an ordinary knife to cut, it was up to me, the Green Witch, to keep them under control. Once again I was on my hands and knees, bumping my head and banging my elbows as I used magic clippers to trim the ever-growing vines.

Being the Green Witch meant that I had a lot of extra

responsibilities. Although I was the most powerful witch in Greater Greensward, as well as its only princess, most of the things I had to do as its protector were neither glamorous nor exciting. At least I didn't have to clean out the moat very often, a job I really hated.

I was reaching for the next curling vine when a bright yellow butterfly landed on my finger and fluttered its wings as if trying to get my attention. "What do you want?" I asked.

The butterfly stomped its feet with impatience. I raised my finger to my ear and tried to listen, but couldn't hear anything over the usual early morning bustle of the Great Hall. Squires were cleaning their knights' weapons while flirting with passing maids. My father's hounds were scuffling over a bone in the corner. The steward was directing the hanging of new banners along the walls.

I could hardly hear the tiny insect, but then I remembered that their voices were extremely soft. Hearing them requires a magic spell, undivided attention, and a very keen ear. I'd had enough practice creating my own spells that coming up with one to hear the butterfly was easy.

Although I'd never spoken with a butterfly before, I expected its voice to be sweet. Instead it sounded like an old man who was hoarse from shouting. "Take your time, lady," said the butterfly. "I don't have anything better to do—just flit from flower to flower until I've inspected every one in that garden. It shouldn't take me much longer than, say . . . my entire life! So, what's it going to be? Are you going to see the old lady or not?"

"Who are you talking about?"

"I knew you weren't paying attention. I could be back at work doing something important, but no, I had to carry a message to someone who can't even be bothered to listen!"

"I'm sorry. I couldn't hear you. What was your message?"

"I don't have time for this! The old lady with the roses wants me to tell you that she's going to work on her house today. She wants to know if you're going to come help. That's it. That's all I know. If you'll answer her question, I'll be on my way. I have a lot of flying ahead of me, so if you don't mind . . ."

"Yes, I'll be there. You have your answer—now go."

A shadow loomed over me as the butterfly zigzagged across the Great Hall and up to one of the windows. "What was that all about?" demanded my mother, who had slipped up behind me.

I sighed and turned around. Although the removal of the family curse had made my grandmother and aunt sweet and kind again, it hadn't done a thing for my mother. She hadn't been affected by the curse, so she was the same as she'd always been. It didn't matter to her that I was the Green Witch and sixteen years old; she still treated me as if I were five. The only time she listened to what I had to say was when I turned into a dragon, and then *everyone* paid attention to me. Most of the time, she tried to tell me what to do while I tried to avoid her.

If I'd been thinking clearly, I might have given her some excuse, but instead I made the mistake of telling her the truth. "I told Grandmother to let me know when she was going to work on her cottage. She sent word that she's about to start."

"So you're going to the Old Witches' Retirement Community? Then we can ride in my carriage together. I was planning to go see her today anyway."

"Ride?" I said, adding the vine clippings to the pile I'd already started. I hadn't ridden in a carriage for months, because I hated the jostling and bumping and now had other ways to get around. As the Green Witch I toured Greater Greensward on my magic carpet every few weeks. When I wasn't using the carpet, I generally flew another way, as a bird, a bat, or a dragon, although being a dragon was the most fun.

"I was just about to leave," I said. "If you have something to do first, you can come when you're ready." I was still hoping that I could go by myself. The Old Witches' Retirement Community was only a few minutes away if I went as a dragon, leaving me enough time to stretch my wings and soar above the clouds and . . .

"I'm ready now," said Mother. "You won't get out of it that easily."

It had been almost two months since I'd learned how to turn myself into a dragon. I'd done it out of necessity at the end of the tournament held to celebrate my sixteenth birthday. My grandmother and aunt had gotten into a magical argument, and I'd had to turn myself into the biggest, fiercest creature that I could think of to get them to listen. Since then I'd taken to saying the spell so often that the people of Greater Greensward had grown used to seeing a green dragon soaring overhead. I liked being a dragon because it made me feel stronger and freer than I'd ever felt before. As a dragon, I could also fly farther and faster than in any other form I'd ever tried.

Unfortunately, traveling with my mother meant that I wasn't going to get a chance to be anything but my human self. She never had wanted me to do magic, although she had gotten used to it after I proved that I had the talent. Recently, we'd formed a sort of unspoken truce; she wouldn't tell me how awful magic was and I wouldn't use it around her unless it was absolutely necessary, but there was always the chance that one of us might forget and slip. Because this made our relationship even more strained and uncomfortable than it had been already, being in a confined space with her for any length of time was one of the last things I wanted to do.

The ride was worse than I'd feared; a heavy rain the night before had scoured large ruts in the roads, and of course my mother refused to let me use my magic to do anything about them. She and I both knew that I would eventually be the one to fix them, just not while she was there. We were well inside the enchanted forest on the road to Grandmother's cottage when we hit a bad bump and I thumped my head against the side of the carriage.

Mother clicked her tongue and said, "I suppose you're going to tell me that you'd rather be flying. Don't bother," she added when I opened my mouth to speak. "I know you don't like spending time with me. You never have. You always preferred my sister's company over mine, and who could blame you? Her responsibilities were exciting, whereas I had the boring and thankless job of supervising the running of a castle. And now that you're safeguarding the kingdom with your magic, you have even less time for me."

"I didn't know that you . . ."

"Of course you didn't," she snapped. "You never think about how I feel. I just hope that when you have a daughter, she considers your feelings more than you have mine and shows you more respect as well. I know you think I'm foolish and don't know what I'm talking about, but I'm right far more often than you think I am."

"I never . . ."

"It would serve you well to start listening to me. Ah, here we are," she said, leaning forward to peer out the window. "I hope your grandmother has the presence of mind to let me choose the candy for those shutters. Oh, dear, is that my father? I thought he was still at the castle."

"He is moving in with her," I reminded my mother.

She sighed and sat back in her seat. "I know and there isn't a thing I can do about it. It's a very bad idea, if you ask me. She'll catch her death of cold if he stays in her cottage, mark my word!"

My grandmother's cottage was one of the more traditional styles of candy-decorated gingerbread. Since the curse had ended, she often invited the family to visit, and Eadric had grown fond of the icing on her roof. I thought it was only right that I help her patch her house, considering how much of it Eadric had eaten.

Grandmother was waiting by her gate when the carriage rolled to a stop. "Where's my favorite young man?" she asked, craning her neck to look around me as I stepped down. "I made some extra gingerbread for him."

"If you mean Eadric, he went hunting with Emma's father," Mother declared, appearing in the door of the carriage. My mother had long feared that no one would ever ask for my hand, and even though Eadric wanted to marry me, she seemed to resent him, perhaps because she hadn't chosen him herself.

"I'll save it for him then," Grandmother said. "Come see what I've done so far, Emma. I've decided to build an addition. Your grandfather should have some space he can call his own. Oh, good. Here he is now."

A blue haze drifted toward us from the direction of the rosebushes, taking on the vague outline of a man. As it drew closer, it became more distinct until I was able to recognize the ghost of my grandfather King Aldrid. Even so, the sunlight kept him from looking as nearly solid as he did when indoors.

"Hello, my dears," he said in a whispery voice. "It's a pleasure to see you."

We shivered at his approach. Grandmother pulled her shawl more closely around her shoulders and smiled up at him. "I'll go see about the candy," Mother said, backing away. Glancing at her father's ghost, she hurried around the corner.

"I'm sorry I disturb her so," said Grandfather.

Grandmother shook her head. "It isn't your fault, dearest. Chartreuse was the first to hear about your death from the banshee and took it very hard. It was difficult for her to accept that you'd come back as a ghost."

Everyone knew that my mother was afraid of ghosts. For years she had claimed that she didn't believe in them, a convenient reason for not visiting her own father, who spent most of his time in the dungeon. However, everyone had seen him kiss my grandmother, thereby ending the family curse. Mother could no longer pretend that he didn't exist. Even so, she tried to avoid his company, claiming that the chill of his ghostly presence gave her the sniffles.

Once the curse had ended and Grandmother was once again her sweet self, Mother visited her more often. "Making up for lost time," she called it. I wondered if she would still come around after Grandfather moved in.

While Grandmother and I fetched the cooled slabs of gingerbread, my mother stayed inside the cottage, collecting the candy. One of the community rules stated that the occupants had to repair their cottages themselves without the use of magic or hired hands, although they could get friends or relatives to help. This seemed odd in a community where many of the cottages walked around on chicken legs and the magic was so thick at times that the air seemed alive with it. I think it was meant to promote community spirit, but whatever the reason, it meant that even the older witches residing there remained active.

We were setting the first slab of gingerbread in place when Grandfather said, "Has Eadric heard from his parents? They were so angry when they left."

Grandmother shook her head. "I still can't believe that woman said those things. She had a lot of nerve, calling Emma a horrid little witch and all those other awful names. They suited me, not you," she said, glancing in my direction.

"Those names don't suit you anymore," I said. "And I hope that isn't how she feels about me now. After his parents left, Eadric wrote to her, telling her how much he loves me. She's my future mother-in-law—at least I want her to be."

Grandmother gave me a sharp look. "You're not going to let her stand in the way of your marriage, are you? The women in our family have more spine than that!"

"I'm still going to marry Eadric. It's just that I'd rather do it with his parents' blessing. I don't think his father hates me like his mother does, but he didn't seem too happy that I'm a witch. And didn't you hear Queen Frazzela say that they'd pass Eadric over and give his brother, Bradston, the crown if Eadric married me?"

"Do you really think they'd do that?"

"I don't know, but I'd rather not take the chance. His whole life Eadric has been planning to rule Upper Montevista. I don't want to be the one to stand in his way. And can you imagine what an awful king Bradston would make?"

My mother had returned carrying a basket of gumdrops, but I noticed that she was careful to stay as far as possible from my grandfather. "I told you that taking an interest in magic was a bad idea," she said. "If you hadn't started practicing, she wouldn't have had anything to complain about."

"Don't be silly, Chartreuse," said Grandmother. "I didn't raise you to be so shortsighted. If Emma hadn't shown an interest in magic, your sister, Grassina, and I would still be under the influence of that awful curse and

I wouldn't have my Aldrid back. Frazzela is just too muzzy-headed to recognize a gem when she sees it. Our little Emma would make anyone proud."

"I couldn't agree more," said Grandfather. "Why, I remember when Emma was trying to find Hubert's medallion and . . ."

A sparrow darted through the garden, skimming the tops of Grandmother's roses. It landed on the rock-candy sundial and twittered a greeting. Herald, Grandmother's orange tabby, licked his lips and wiggled his back end as he prepared to pounce. As the sparrow opened his beak, Herald twitched his tail and leaped.

"Not so fast," said Grandfather, thrusting out his arm and waving his fingers. A wind sprang up that only the cat could feel, blowing him midleap into the rosebushes. Yowling, Herald clawed his way out of the roses and took off across the yard. Grandfather chuckled. "I don't think that cat likes me."

The sparrow bobbed its head. "Your Highnesses," it said. "Lady Grassina requests the pleasure of your company in the swamp behind the castle. She says that Princess Emeralda will know where to go." Having delivered its message, the sparrow took off, going back the way it had come. Grassina must have used a spell on the bird to make it speak the human tongue, because even my mother had looked as if she could understand what it was saying.

Grandmother had been smoothing icing with her hand before attaching the first gumdrop. "What do you suppose she wants?" she said, wiping her fingers on her apron.

When I saw that they were all looking my way, I shrugged. "I have no idea. She hasn't told me a thing."

"Does she expect us to go now?" asked my mother. "She can't order us around. We're in the middle of this."

"Well, I'm going," announced Grandmother. "I want to see what this is about. Herald, you keep an eye on the house."

An orange-striped tail dangled from the leafy branch of a crab-apple tree at the edge of the yard. The only sign that Herald had heard her was the angry twitch of the tip of his tail.

My mother dropped the gumdrops she was holding back into the basket. "If you're going, there's no use in the rest of us staying here. We'll take my carriage."

"I prefer to fly," said Grandmother.

"And leave me to ride by myself? I thought you liked my company, Mother."

Grandmother sighed. "Of course I do, Chartreuse."

"Then that's settled. We'll all take the carriage, except, er, Father, if you don't mind . . ."

"Don't worry, Chartreuse. I know there isn't room for me."

Two

The ride to the swamp was only slightly less unpleasant than the ride to the cottage had been. The driver of the coach was more familiar with the changes in the road and was able to miss some of the deeper ruts. Although my mother didn't say anything at first, I knew that the spots of color on her normally pale cheeks meant that she was angry.

"Doesn't it bother you that Grassina is being so inconsiderate?" she finally blurted.

My grandmother had looked composed with her hands folded in her lap as she gazed out the window. When she turned to face us, she seemed surprised at the question. "Why, no, not at all. I'm sure that your sister wouldn't have asked us to come on a whim. I don't know why she wants us there, but whatever it is, it must be important."

The spots on Mother's cheeks flamed as she bit her lip. "You're taking her side, just the way you did when we were girls."

Grandmother nodded. "Yes, I am, but I take your side when you aren't around and your sister questions something that you do. I always give my girls the benefit of the doubt. I'm sorry the curse turned me into a horrible mother for all those years."

"You take my side, too?" my mother said as if that was all she'd heard.

"Of course," said Grandmother. "You just aren't there to hear it."

"Oh," Mother said. Although she didn't speak again until we reached the swamp, the bright spots faded from her cheeks.

I understood why Grassina had said that I would know the place she meant. My aunt and I were the only people from the castle who visited the swamp, and we'd been exploring it for years. But if this was as important as her summons made it seem, there was only one place we'd find her. She'd be at the pond where I'd first met Eadric and where she had changed Haywood from an otter back into a human.

We left the coach at the road as close as we could get to the swamp and walked the rest of the way. My mother was horrified, of course, because it meant getting her shoes dirty. She tried to keep her hem out of the muck when we reached soggier ground, but she didn't have much luck and finally gave up altogether, letting her hem drag wherever it would.

I was pleased to see that I was right about Grassina's choice. She was waiting where I'd thought she'd be, with Haywood at her side. Eadric and my father were there, as well as another man I'd never seen before. It wasn't until I saw that he was wearing priest's robes that I began to understand why we'd been summoned.

The ceremony was lovely. Grassina and Haywood stood before Father Alphonse at the edge of the water while the rest of us watched from farther up the bank. Although she wore one of her ordinary moss-green gowns, had a simple wreath of ivy in her hair, and carried a plain bouquet of daisies, the glow of happiness that lit Grassina's face made her as lovely as any bride had ever looked. Haywood was wearing one of the tunics my aunt had embroidered for him. It was decorated with oak leaves and acorns in dark greens and warm browns that seemed remarkably lifelike. He looked proud and happy standing beside Grassina, reminding me of the expression he'd worn when he was an enchanted otter and they had just found each other again.

As far as I was concerned, only one thing marred the ceremony: my mother wouldn't stop complaining. Although she stood on the other side of Eadric and my grandparents, I could hear every word she said, and none of it was nice. I glanced at the rest of my family. From their expressions, my father seemed to be the only other person who could hear my mother's tirade. Unfortunately, I could hear her as clearly as the grasshoppers chirping in the field behind us, the birds calling in the trees across the river, the fish burbling in the river, and . . . It occurred to me that I hadn't undone the spell allowing me to hear the butterfly. Maybe that was why everything seemed so loud.

"She's so inconsiderate—having her wedding in a swamp!" said my mother as the priest talked about love and marriage. "What a deplorable site for a wedding ceremony! Demanding we go to this godforsaken place just because . . . Do you smell that? I just know this is a breeding ground for the plague. What is that on my shoe? Ooh, I think it's moving!"

I saw my father lower his head toward hers. "It's a slug, my dear. It won't hurt you."

"And do you, Haywood, take Grassina as your lawfully wedded wife?" said Father Alphonse.

"And calling us here at the very last minute! She had to have known how much planning her wedding would have meant to me. If she'd given me fair warning, I could have had a dress made for her and a feast prepared. I could have sent out invitations, had the castle cleaned, gotten her a gift. . . . It's her fault that no one will have

16

presents for her. If she'd waited a few days, although a week or two would have been better . . ."

"There, there, Chartreuse," said my father. "I'm sure she'll understand."

"*. . . as long as you both shall live,*" *said the priest.*

Glancing pointedly at Queen Olivene and the ghost of my grandfather, my mother added, "And after they die, too, if they're anything like my parents."

At least they have a good marriage, I thought, remembering how often my parents had refused to talk to each other when I was growing up.

Eadric squeezed my hand. "What a great wedding," he whispered to me as Grassina and Haywood exchanged rings. "I'd like a simple wedding like this. I could talk to the priest after the ceremony and ask him to stick around to do ours. We could even have it here in the swamp, if that's what you really want."

"We can't," I said, although I would have liked nothing better. "I want to get your parents' blessing first. If we're going to get married, I want to do it right."

"I don't think they're going to give it," said Eadric. "You know what they were like when they left, and they never did reply to my letter."

"That's why I want to get their blessing. I don't want to cause a rift between you and your parents."

"If there's any rift, they were the ones who made it."

"Eadric, I mean it. Blessing first, then the wedding."

17

"All right, if we have to," he said, but he didn't look happy about it. "We'll go see them as soon as we can. I don't want to put off our wedding any longer."

"... *man and wife*," *said Father Alphonse*.

Grassina and Haywood kissed and everyone watched in silence. When they pulled away to look into each other's eyes, someone sobbed softly. I realized that my mother was crying.

We were starting to line up to congratulate the bride and groom when I heard splashing behind us in the swamp. Whoever it was seemed to be having a terrible time, tripping and falling, then swearing when he tried to get up. When I turned to see who it was, Eadric's eyes followed mine and his hand immediately flew to Ferdy, his singing sword. It was one of my father's guards slogging through the taller grass with his sodden hat in one hand and a mud-covered shoe in the other. He was pouring water out of the shoe when he stopped in front of my father, but he must have forgotten about it because he slapped himself in the face with it when he tried to salute. Sputtering, he used his sleeve to wipe muddy water from his eyes, then said, "Your Majesty, I've come to report that Prince Jorge has escaped from the dungeon. He was there when the guard last checked, but he's gone now and the door is still locked from the outside. I was stationed by the dungeon door, and I swear no one got past me."

"He must have bribed someone in the castle to let

him out," growled my father. "When I find out who it was, I'll . . ."

"Actually, he could have gotten out any number of ways," said my grandmother. "And before you start threatening to lop off someone's head, why don't you let Emma and me take a look. I'm sure that between the two of us we can learn what actually happened."

Father nodded, aware of how useful a little magic might be, but from the look in his eyes I knew that if we couldn't find the answer, someone was bound to pay the price.

Eadric, too, looked grim. It was because of him that Jorge was in the dungeon. The prince hadn't been pleased that I'd preferred to be in the swamp rather than with him. Because I wouldn't marry Jorge, his father, King Beltran, had led his army into war against Greater Greensward. With Eadric's help, I'd used my magic to end the war, but Jorge still wasn't satisfied. When my father held the tournament for my sixteenth birthday, the prince had shown up disguised as one of the contestants and had done his best to kill Eadric. Fortunately, a health and safety spell had foiled his plan, and Jorge had been thrown into my father's dungeon.

Of course, the dungeon wasn't quite like it used to be. My mother had had it cleaned out when she married my father and had used it for storage since then. The guards had scrambled to get a cell ready for a prisoner, finally settling on one with a tiny window. The cell had been used to house old furniture in need of repair and was cluttered, but dry and relatively clean. Rather than make him wait while they emptied it completely, they'd left a few pieces behind. A cracked washtub, a rickety table, and my old bed with the broken leg weren't much, but they were more than most prisoners had.

We'd never intended to keep him there for long because custom decreed that the prince be released as soon as his ransom was paid. Although my father sent word to King Beltran that his son was in our dungeon, the old king was too stingy to send his ransom. Two months later the prince was still in the cell, gaining weight from Cook's good food and taunting the ghosts who dared stop in.

Although Father and Eadric both looked upset, I almost welcomed the news that Jorge had escaped. I'd been avoiding the dungeon for as long as he was in residence, and I missed my forays down there to visit my ghostly friends. Unfortunately, I knew that if Jorge were loose, he'd be up to no good as soon as he got the chance.

While my parents stayed to talk to the newlyweds, Grandmother and I went to the dungeon. Eadric and my grandfather insisted on going, too, which was just as well, because some of the shyer ghosts wouldn't talk to anyone except another ghost. We found the dungeon just as the guard had described. The door was locked from the outside, the straw mattress rumpled but unoccupied. While Eadric checked under the bed and in the washtub to make sure that Jorge wasn't hiding, I looked around for magical clues. Like most other things, magic leaves a kind of residue for those who know how to find it. Holding my hand out to feel for the energy, I wasn't surprised to find that magic had been used there in the very recent past.

"I found someone to talk to us," said my grandfather, floating back through the door.

Two ghosts followed him into the cell, making the space unbearably cold. I shivered and moved closer to Eadric's warmth while my grandmother pulled her wrap tight around her shoulders. I recognized both of the ghosts as acquaintances of my grandfather's to whom he had introduced me before. One was Hubert, the ghost of an elderly servant who had been thrown into the oubliette to die. He still wore the ghostly chain around his neck, less tarnished than the real one that had been buried along with his bones after the skeletons in the dungeon helped us. His companion was Sir Jarvis, a gentleman of the court from some century past whose noble bearing offset Hubert's aged stoop. The difference in their status would have kept them apart when they were alive, but as ghosts they had become the closest of friends.

"Do I know you?" Hubert said, peering up at me through his straggly hair.

"Of course you do, old man," said Sir Jarvis, patting Hubert's arm. "It's King Aldrid's granddaughter, Princess Emma. You met her a few months back, don't you remember?"

"No!" snapped Hubert. "Never met her before. Nor any of these other people. Although I'd like to meet this one," he said, winking at my white-haired grandmother.

My grandfather's outline seemed to grow until his head looked like it was about to touch the ceiling. "That is my wife, Queen Olivene!"

"Beg pardon, sir," said Hubert, cowering as he probably had when he was alive. "Didn't mean to offend."

"And no offense will be taken as long as you can provide us with some answers," said my grandmother. "Tell us, were either of you near this cell earlier today?"

"I wasn't, Your Majesty," said Sir Jarvis, "but Hubert might have been."

"Maybe I was," Hubert said, suddenly shifty-eyed. "Why do you want to know?"

Grandfather loomed over Hubert, making the servant's ghost shrink back. "The prisoner in this cell escaped a short time ago. We want to find out how he did it."

"Don't know anything about that," Hubert said, sounding defensive. "Didn't see any man leave."

"This isn't getting us anywhere," said Eadric.

"Just what did you see?" I asked the ghost.

Hubert shrugged. "Saw one man arrive in a puff of

smoke, he did. A bit later two birds flew out the window, *fft,* right between the bars like that!" he said, brushing his hands together.

"And did you hear what they said?" asked my grandfather.

"I don't know! I guess they chirped like most birds do. What kind of question is that? I want to go now. Asking questions about chirping birds!" Muttering to himself, Hubert drifted from the room, leaving Sir Jarvis to apologize.

"So they left as birds," said Eadric. "At least that's something."

I nodded. "I just wish we knew who came to help Jorge."

"There's a hamster," said Grandfather, pointing at a furry little creature scurrying along a narrow ledge. "Maybe it knows what happened."

The dungeon was overrun with hamsters that had been spiders until Grassina cast a spell to change every one of them. They were shy and skittish, so I didn't hold much hope that the hamster would talk to me. When I bent down to talk to this one, it gave a high-pitched squeal and fell off the ledge. Thinking that it might be hurt, I reached down to pick it up, but it limped away before I could catch it.

"I'd leave it alone if I were you," said my grandmother from the doorway. "You'll only frighten it more. Look who I found," she said, holding out her cupped hands and opening them to reveal a fuzzy rat. It was Blister, Grassina's rat from when she'd made her home in the dungeon. My aunt's magic dust had made its fur grow long and silky. My suggestion along with one of her spells had made it unable to speak unless it had something nice to say. The rat didn't usually say much anymore.

"Oh, you found *him*," I said.

Blister turned his head my way only after hearing my voice. "You would be here, wouldn't you?" he muttered.

"We want to ask you a question," I said. "Did you see what happened in this cell today?"

"You're asking me?" said the rat. "I can't see a thing through all this hair. And it's your fault. If you weren't such a . . ." Blister stopped talking.

"Don't bother with him," I told Grandmother when she glared at the rat. "He wouldn't help us even if he could. I wish there were someone else we could ask. I'd love to know what Jorge said."

"If only walls had ears," said Eadric to himself.

He grunted when I turned and flung my arms around him. "That's it!" I said. "You are so brilliant! You've given me the best idea. How about this . . ."

> If walls had ears to hear,
> And also mouths to speak,
> Imagine what they'd say
> If they weren't quite so meek.

Please give this wall a chance
To tell us what it heard
When Jorge left this room.
(We know he was a bird.)

We all waited, half expecting the wall to say something profound. When it didn't say anything at all, I tapped it with my finger and said, "Well, don't you have anything to say?"

"No," said the wall. "Leave me alone."

I couldn't have been more surprised. "Really? You finally have the opportunity to talk and you don't want to?"

"That's right," it said. "Now go away."

"All right," I said. "We will, just as soon as you answer our questions."

"What if I don't want to?"

"Then we'll stay right here until you do."

"What do you want to know?" it asked in a grudging kind of voice.

"We want to know who you saw in this room today," said Eadric.

"That's easy. I saw a human with yellow hair and blue eyes. He was here most of the day. . . . He has been every day since I first saw him. Then there was this funny crackling sound, and a shorter human appeared with lots of hair on his face and none on the top of his head. The first human shouted at him, 'It took you long enough.' Then the hairy-faced human said, 'I'm sorry, Your Majesty. I just got off the island. I came here as soon as I heard what had happened.' The yellow-haired human stomped his foot and shouted, 'Well, don't just stand there, fool. Get me out of this dung heap!' Then the hairy-faced man waved his hand and they both turned into birds."

Eadric turned to look at me. "It was Olebald, wasn't it?"

"It must have been," I said. "That means he finally got off the island where I sent him. This can't be good."

"They were interesting," said the wall, "but not nearly as much fun to watch as the man who thought he was a bat. He was here for years before he got the idea that he could hang upside down from the ceiling. I don't know how many times he landed on his head."

Eadric's eyes looked grim and his jaw had tightened the way it does when he's really angry. "If Jorge's loose, we're leaving tomorrow morning for Upper Montevista. We'll go see my parents and get their blessing so we can get married before Jorge can do anything else. If I know him, all he can think about now is what rotten thing he can do to prevent our wedding."

"You can't leave now!" said the wall. "I have so much I want to tell you. Why just the other year . . ."

Grabbing my arm, Eadric hustled me out of the cell. We could still hear the wall talking as we left the dungeon. I considered staying behind to undo the spell, but I didn't quite have the heart.

26

Three

After eating a breakfast of bread and cheese with Eadric, I returned to my tower to get ready for our flight to Upper Montevista. We would be leaving as soon as Eadric came back from seeing his horse. Although we planned to be gone only a few days, Eadric was too fond of Bright Country to leave without saying good-bye.

I spread my magic carpet in front of the window and was watching a broom sweep it clean when I heard a knock on the door and an unmistakable voice said, "I know you're in there, Emeralda. Open the door this instant."

I ground my teeth, irritated that my mother could still make me feel like a child. Although I would have loved to pretend that I wasn't there, I decided to be mature and let her in. Hating myself already, I opened the door and stepped aside.

"There you are," she said, pushing past me into the room. "I heard that you intend to . . ."

I knew when her eyes fell on the sweeping broom

that it was all she would need to set her off. Kicking my-self inwardly, I twitched my fingers, sending the broom into the storage room.

"You can't resist, can you?" she said, her eyes narrow-ing. "You use magic for even a simple task like sweeping. I'm so disappointed, Emeralda. You always have to take the easy way out. Would it really have been that much more difficult to summon a maid to do it?"

I dug my nails into the palm of my hand, trying not to answer the way I really wanted to. Arguing with her only made things worse. "Did you want to talk to me about something?" I said, my voice as even as I could make it.

"As I was saying, I heard that you intend to go to Up-per Montevista to visit Eadric's parents. Am I correct in assuming that you're going to talk to them about your wedding plans?"

I nodded. "Eadric and I hope to receive their bless-ing before we get married."

"And you want to take that," she said, glaring at the magic carpet before turning to me with a disgusted look on her face. "Don't be a fool! That should be the last thing you'd want to do. If Eadric's parents are as ap-palled that you're a witch as I believe they are, don't you think it might be wise to travel in a more traditional man-ner? Rubbing their noses in the very thing that they dis-like about you is not a good way to win their favor."

I hated that she was right. "I suppose," I said.

"Then put that *thing* away and decide what you want to take with you. You'll be traveling with the best carriages and a full retinue. I'll see to the arrangements. You'll have to inform Eadric, of course, and choose enough clothes to last at least a week on the road. You'll also want to take your nicer gowns so you can make a good impression when you arrive. I'll send a maid up to help you."

"You don't need to do that," I said, but she had already disappeared down the stairs.

I always cleaned my tower myself because I didn't like the idea of anyone touching my magical possessions. The same held true for packing, so it didn't matter if my mother sent someone to help me; I wouldn't be letting her in.

I was rolling up the carpet when Li'l fluttered out of the storage room and landed on my worktable. "Your mother is just the same as ever, isn't she? Are you going to do what she said?"

"I guess I have to. She was right about Eadric's parents, so I really don't have much choice."

"Can I go with you?" the little bat asked. "Garrid is going to be gone for a while, and I don't have anyplace else to go." Garrid, a vampire, was her mate.

"You could stay here if you want to. The door will be locked and no one will bother you."

Li'l's head drooped and her voice grew soft. "But I'll be all alone. I've never been all alone before."

29

"You might find that you like it," I said. Then she heaved an enormous sigh and I couldn't help myself. "But you can come if you want to." After all, I was supposed to go with an entourage, and I really didn't have that many people I wanted to take.

"Oh, goody!" said Li'l, flapping her wings and rising into the air to circle around my head. "Goody, goody, goody, I get to go! I've never been in a carriage before. Your mother said that you should take clothes. Should I take something, too? I could take my string, or some nice bugs. Will we sleep in the carriage or under a tree? Does the carriage have rafters? Will I have to stay awake while the carriage is moving? We're going to have so much fun!"

I was getting dizzy from watching her. "You won't need to bring a thing," I said, laughing. "I'm sure you'll find plenty of nice bugs along the way."

"Along the way where?" said Eadric. I'd changed the spell on the door lock so it would let him in, although he usually knocked first.

"It looks like we're going to have to change our plans," I began.

Eadric scowled. "Yes, I know. Your mother told me."

"I'm going, too!" said Li'l. "Emma said I could."

"Huh," said Eadric. "At least someone is excited about this trip."

"Here," I said, handing him the rolled-up carpet. "Could you put this away for me?"

Eadric grinned. "As long as you pay the fee."

"All right. I'll even pay in advance." Hooking my finger into the neck of Eadric's tunic, I pulled him toward me and kissed him squarely on the lips.

"Yuck! Do you two have to do that in front of me?" asked Li'l, landing on the table and covering her eyes with her wings.

"You mean bats don't kiss?" Eadric asked.

"Not like that!" said Li'l, turning her back to us.

Suddenly, I heard a sloshing sound. A light like a shooting star whooshed from the bowl of salt water I kept by the door, hitting the floor on the other side of the room and depositing a beautiful, full-sized mermaid with slanted dark blue eyes and pale skin tinged with green.

"*Oof!*" said the mermaid, landing on her tail. "I never can get used to that."

"Coral!" I said. "Is that you?"

"Hi, Emma!" she replied, flinging her mass of blue-streaked silver hair over her shoulder and scattering droplets of water everywhere.

Coral was one of Grassina's friends whom I'd once visited. A tiny castle rested in the bottom of the bowl, but it wasn't until I had swum in the salt water myself that I'd known it was the mermaid's home and part of the ocean. I didn't know that she could come visit us as well. "It's good to see you," I said, not sure why she was here.

"You, too, but I really can't stay. I've come to ask you for a favor."

"Of course," I said. "I'll do whatever I can." She'd helped Eadric and me when we needed her, and I couldn't say no.

Her eyes lit up as she thrust a hand into her hair. "I was hoping you'd say that," she said, pulling out something green and squirmy. "I'm on my way to visit my friend and she's allergic to shellfish, so I was wondering if Shelton could stay with you until I get back. I'd leave him with Octavius, but they can't seem to get along."

"That's because he's a pinheaded nitwit," said the little green crab as he scuttled down the mermaid's arm to the floor. "He keeps threatening to rip off my shell and feed me to the sharks."

Coral sighed. "You did tie his arms in knots."

"Only after he wrapped me in seaweed and stuffed me in the trash!"

"See what I mean?" Coral said, shaking her head.

"Actually, we were about to go on a trip ourselves," said Eadric. "So maybe this isn't the best time for . . ."

"We'd be delighted to have Shelton stay with us," I interrupted. Magical beings were easily offended, and it was always better to stay on their good side. Unfortunately, Octavius, Coral's octopus butler, wasn't the only one who found Shelton annoying. The little crab had bickered with Eadric from the moment they'd met.

32

"Then it's all settled!" exclaimed the mermaid. Blowing a kiss to Shelton, she drew a silver comb from her hair and pulled it through the strands. "Thank you!" she called as she began to glow. A moment later, she was so bright that we couldn't look at her, and with a whoosh and a splash, she was back in the tank.

"Hey," said Eadric. "We had to stick our hand in the water before we could go into the bowl!"

I shrugged. "Maybe it was easier for her because she was already wet."

"So Princess," said Shelton, "how have you been? I'm doing fine, in case you want to know." Shelton swiveled his eyestalks toward Eadric. "Better than you, I guess, since *he's* still around. Say, that otter isn't here, is he? I've been having bad dreams about him."

"Grassina turned him back into a human," I said.

Eadric chuckled. "Too bad, huh?"

"Please don't get started, you two." The trip was already going to be too long. If I was going to have any peace at all, I'd have to keep the two of them separated, but that might not always be possible if we were traveling together. And Eadric was already unhappy about our change of plans. . . .

"Shelton," I said when Eadric had left the room to get his things. "Perhaps you should stay here while we're gone. We'll be away only a few days. We're going to travel by coach, which you probably wouldn't like anyway."

The little crab's eyestalks drooped. "You mean you don't want me to go with you? I thought you liked me, Princess."

"I do, Shelton, but that isn't the point. We're going to be very busy, and I won't always be able to spend time with you."

"I understand," said Shelton, looking even more dejected.

I tried not to look at him while I chose the things that I would take with me. Space wasn't a problem because I'd recently purchased an acorn trunk at the magic market-place. Although it looked like a regular acorn, it could hold just about anything. I had yet to learn if it had any limits.

It took me only a few minutes to pack my clothes. When I was ready, I stuffed my acorn in the pouch I wear on my hip and headed for the stairs.

Li'l had never liked my mother and always tried to stay out of sight when she was around. Instead of going through the castle with me, the little bat flew out the window and went straight to the first carriage waiting in the courtyard. When I arrived, Eadric was there with Bright Country saddled and ready.

"Let's get going before my mother makes us take everybody in the castle," I told Eadric.

"Do you want to ride with me?" he asked. The few times we'd gone anywhere on horseback, we'd ridden Bright Country together. The stallion was a destrier, bred for carrying knights in full suits of armor, so carrying Eadric and me in ordinary clothes was easy for him.

"I'd love to," I said, taking his hand. Eadric hauled me up behind him, turning Brighty toward the gate. "We're ready to go now," I called to the coachman, who was watching us open-mouthed. Although my mother had a row of coaches ready and waiting, I hoped we could take just one and still avoid a large entourage.

"Very good, Your Highness," he said, although I noticed that he'd raised an eyebrow.

Brighty hadn't taken more than a few steps when my mother came rushing out the castle door followed by a dozen knights, a flock of servants, and two ladies-in-waiting. "Stop right there," she commanded, glowering at me. "I knew you'd do something like this! I told you that you needed a full retinue and I'm going to see that you get one, even if you don't think it's necessary."

My mother had been right about the carpet, but I hated traveling with large groups of people. I'd done it, of course, when I'd gone places with my parents. My mother never traveled any distance without taking half the court. With so many people, however, we couldn't travel very fast or far in one day, and we had to take so many extra carriages and food and luggage that it felt as if we were moving an army. And forget about being spontaneous. My mother always planned everything in advance, so if it wasn't already scheduled, we didn't do it.

Mother hurried across the courtyard to where we still sat astride Bright Country. "So, you weren't even going to take a carriage?"

"Actually, one was supposed to follow us," I said, feeling sheepish.

Mother sniffed. "You have your own palfrey to ride if you want to enjoy the fresh air. I expect you to conduct yourself with decorum, which is why I selected two ladies-in-waiting to travel with you." She nodded toward the women waiting behind her. I knew both of them, of course, although not very well.

The older woman curtseyed first. "Your Highness," she said. It was Hortense, one of my mother's older ladies-in-waiting. Everyone knew better than to do anything unseemly when Hortense was around for fear of receiving one of her famous tongue-lashings. I'd always suspected that one of Hortense's duties was to act as my mother's spy.

The other lady-in-waiting curtseyed so low that she had a hard time getting back up. Her name was Lucy, and she was the plumpest of my mother's ladies as well as the best at doing my mother's hair. My mother never traveled without Lucy, so I was surprised she was sending her with me. "Your Highness," Lucy said, panting from exertion.

"These ladies will accompany you. Even so," Mother said, looking thoughtful, "I don't think this is enough. To make the right impression, one must be impressive."

"Mother, I'm not waiting for anyone else. Eadric and I want to get started today."

"And you will. The rest will leave tomorrow. Your father is busy or he'd have come to see you off. Be careful on the road and listen to your ladies. They can advise you on etiquette in foreign courts."

"Of course, Mother," I said. *Why hadn't Eadric and I left sooner?* "But if I have to have more people along, I'll take an extra carriage. I'd prefer to ride alone in mine."

"If you must," my mother conceded.

Hortense and Lucy climbed into the second carriage while I slipped off Bright Country's back. The horse whuffled my hair as I patted his neck, knowing that no matter how uncomfortable riding him might have been, the carriage was going to be much worse.

I glanced at the palfrey my mother had mentioned. She was tethered to another horse that one of the servants was riding and seemed like a nice enough mare, but I didn't know her and didn't feel like getting acquainted just then. Instead, I climbed into the first carriage and sat back with a sigh.

"Hi!" said Li'l once the door was shut. Carriages don't have rafters as she'd hoped they would, but the little bat had found purchase for her claws and was hanging upside down in the corner. "Isn't this exciting! I can't wait to get started."

The carriage moved with a jolt, making Li'l sway

back and forth. "Then it looks like you got your wish," I said, feeling glum. My mother wasn't happy because I didn't have a full complement of escorts. I wasn't happy because my mother had been right about one thing and now I was stuck with so many people. And as for Eadric, well, at least he had a horse he liked and didn't have to ride in a carriage.

We hadn't quite reached the gate when someone shouted and the carriage rolled to a stop. "Now what?" I said, sticking my head out the window.

"When you get back, we'll plan a lovely wedding for you," my mother called from the steps to the castle. "Your father still has to arrange the wedding contract, so we'll have plenty of time to make all the necessary arrangements."

"Great," I said, waving good-bye. Settling back in my seat, I closed my eyes and sighed.

Four

We made good time the first day, partly because I refused to make the frequent stops that my mother usually demanded. At least I was the only human in my carriage and didn't have to talk to my mother's hand-picked ladies. Li'l slept most of the morning, dangling from the roof of the carriage like a little black tassel. We had gone only a few miles past the farms surrounding the castle grounds when I felt something crawl onto my lap.

"Oh!" I said when I realized that it was Shelton. He must have hidden in the folds of my gown just as he had on the day that we met. "What are you doing here?"

"I was thinking about what you said. I won't mind if you don't spend all your time with me. I like to travel and see the sights, so you go right ahead and do whatever it is you need to do. If you're going on a long trip, you need me to go with you. You never know when these might prove useful," he said, clacking his claws. "Where are we going anyway?"

I sighed, knowing that I wasn't about to take him back and risk having my mother add to my entourage. "To visit Eadric's parents. They live in Upper Montevista, the kingdom just to the north of Greater Greensward. I've never been there myself, but I hear it's very beautiful."

"Are there any oceans?" asked the little crab.

I shook my head. "No oceans, but there are a lot of mountains."

"That's too bad," he said, and then he scuttled up the wall to the window ledge. "Wow, this thing goes fast!" Grabbing hold with his claws, he fought to keep his balance until I put my hand up to help him.

"I suppose," I said, although a moment before, I'd been thinking how slowly we were moving.

"Where are we now?"

I leaned forward to look out the window. "We're in the enchanted forest. This is the only road that will take us where we want to go. These trees are hundreds of years old."

"Do they have coconuts?" he asked, swiveling his eyestalks toward the tops of the trees. The only trees growing on the island where we'd met had been surrounded by fallen coconuts that the green crabs seemed to love.

"No," I said. "Sorry."

"What are those?" he asked, pointing at a doe and her fawn.

Shelton was interested in everything. After growing up on a tropical island, he had lived on the ocean floor with Coral, so all the things I was used to were new and exciting for him. He was full of questions about the animals, the size of the forest, the way some of the trees pulled up their roots and moved around, and why all the horses screamed and the ladies-in-waiting shrieked when a griffin flew by and I had to say a spell to send it on its way. When we passed a waterfall and saw a green-skinned nymph swimming in the pool at its base, his eyestalks twirled as he asked, "Is that a mermaid?" He was disappointed when I pointed out that she had legs instead of a tail, but he seemed pleased to have seen her at all.

By midafternoon I was already sore from the jolting of the carriage and tired of the stuffy air. Casting a spell on a leather pouch to make it leak-proof, I filled it with water for Shelton and wedged it in the corner of the carriage. The little crab was happily bobbing in the cool water when I had my coachman stop and went to meet the palfrey I'd been given. The dappled gray had been tethered behind the last carriage and left saddled and ready. I introduced myself before climbing onto her back, but she didn't seem interested in me or in the fact that we could talk to each other. I asked her name and learned that it was Gwynnie. She grunted as I settled myself in the saddle, but seemed eager when I asked her to trot toward the front of the line.

"He's so handsome," she said, nodding her head toward Eadric. "All the girls have been talking about him."

Of course I thought Eadric was handsome, but I didn't know that horses looked at people that way, too.

"I've seen you with him around the stables. Do you think you could introduce me?"

"Sure, if that's what you really want."

We trotted past my carriage to where Eadric was riding with some of the knights. He'd stayed in the front most of the day, dropping back only long enough to talk to me or to see how everyone else was doing. I was proud of the way he had taken charge of our expedition, even though traveling this way hadn't been his idea.

When I reached Eadric's side, I smiled at him and said, "I have someone I'd like you to meet. This is Gwynnie."

Gwynnie laid her ears flat against her skull. "I don't want to meet *him*. I meant that good-looking stud the human is riding."

I had to admit, in his silver-trimmed bridle and matching saddle, Eadric's stallion did look very nice. Bright Country pricked his ears at Gwynnie and whinnied hello. She whinnied back, so I knew they'd get along just fine.

"How far are we from Upper Montevista?" I asked Eadric.

"If we keep going at this rate, we'll be there in two or three days. I can't wait for you to see it. It's one of the most beautiful kingdoms in the world. You'll love the mountains. We have the highest peaks and the deepest valleys."

"What about swamps?" I asked. "You know how much I like swamps." I still wanted to get married in one, although I hoped it would be the one back home.

Eadric glanced at me as if I should have known better. "There aren't any swamps in Upper Montevista. That's why I came to Greater Greensward to find the meadwort and happened to meet that witch."

"You mean that when Bradston made up the story about seeing your true love's face in the bottom of a cup of meadwort tea, you came all the way to my kingdom? I didn't know you were gullible enough to go that far."

Eadric gave me a disgusted look. "I prefer to think of it as trusting."

"I've met your little brother. I can't imagine why you'd trust him about something like that."

"Brad can be very convincing when he wants to be," Eadric said, shrugging. "It's how he gets away with so much."

"So what else can you tell me about your kingdom aside from its deplorable lack of swamps? Do you have any enchanted forests?"

"No, but we do have griffins and rocs and trolls in the mountains. On the higher slopes there are other creatures that no one has seen but we know are there by their giant footprints."

"Uh-huh. Are there any other differences that I should know about?"

"We like our food a little spicier in Upper Montevista than in Greater Greensward."

"Oh, really? You never seemed to think that there was anything wrong with our food."

"There isn't," he said, patting his nicely rounded stomach. I don't think Eadric ever met a dish he didn't like.

"Anything else?" I asked.

"Well, yes. I probably should have told you this before: the people of my kingdom aren't as comfortable with magic as the citizens of Greater Greensward are. A lot of my parents' subjects don't like witches."

"You must be extremely open-minded for someone from Upper Montevista."

"I am," he said, looking smug. "But then you've always known that I'm extraordinary."

Gwynnie flicked her ears when I shifted my weight in the saddle. "If your people don't like witches, I'd better not do any magic while I'm there," I said. "I don't want to turn them against me before we even meet."

Eadric frowned. "Are you sure that you can do it? You're used to using magic to take care of things."

"Now you sound like my mother! I don't have to do magic all the time. You'll see."

We rode in silence after that, involved in our own thoughts. I was irritated that no one seemed to think that I could get along without my magic. It was true that it had become an important part of my life, but it wasn't all there was to me. I was a lot more confident than I used to be and more capable and ... I realized that most of what I valued about myself was tied to my magic one way or another. If I couldn't use it, would I be as confident or as capable?

By late afternoon the enchanted forest had given way to the more normal kind, with trees that didn't move around and no creature more frightening than a bear. I was slapping at the flies that couldn't seem to leave Gwynnie alone when a voice shouted, "Hellooo!" and a group of riders appeared through the trees. The man in front was oddly dressed in a leather jerkin and little pointed hat. His beard was trimmed in the middle so that it formed two long curls on either side of his chin. Although the knights who were my escort drew their swords and urged their horses into a protective circle around us, Eadric seemed delighted to see the man.

"He's from Upper Montevista!" said Eadric. "We must be near the border."

Reluctant to sheathe their swords, the knights sat watching the stranger's approach with wary eyes. "Hellooo!" he said again as his horse stopped in the center of the road, forcing us to stop as well. Sweeping his hat from his head, he bowed low in the saddle while smiling broadly at Eadric. "I'm Broadnik Bentwin from Chancewold. We heard that our prince was returning home and hoped that you and your party would honor us by dining in our fair town tonight. It's good to see you back, Your Highness."

Eadric nodded graciously and replied, "We'd be delighted to take you up on your offer, Goodman Bentwin. I've missed a good Montevistian meal these last few months."

I heard a knight chuckle behind me. Apparently my family and the kitchen staff weren't the only ones in the castle who knew about Eadric's appetite.

"That you'll have, Your Highness," said Broadnik. "Along with some excellent entertainment the likes of which you won't get anywhere but our kingdom. Now, if you'll excuse us, we'll be heading home to tell everyone to prepare for your arrival." Twirling his cap on one finger, he set it on his head and turned his horse to face back the way he'd come. With a signal from Broadnik, the other riders turned as well and trotted off into the forest.

"Wasn't that nice?" said Eadric, looking as pleased as if he'd just won a round in a tournament.

"Very," I said, although I wasn't nearly as happy about it. When the knights returned to their places and we could talk without being disturbed, I leaned closer to Eadric. "You could have discussed it with me before telling that man that we'd eat in their town. Do you even know how far away it is? What if we want to stop before then or keep going past it?"

Eadric frowned. "You didn't ask me about changing our plans. You just let your mother tell us what to do."

"But she was right, especially if it's true that the people of Upper Montevista don't like magic. Flying there on a magic carpet would have been a big mistake."

"Maybe," said Eadric. "But you could have talked to me about it before you made up your mind."

I tightened my fingers on the reins, making Gwynnie toss her head and snort. "If you didn't want to do this," I said, "you should have told me."

"I didn't say that I didn't want to do it," said Eadric. "I just meant . . . Never mind."

Eadric and I didn't have much to talk about for a while after that, although Bright Country and Gwynnie continued to nicker as if they'd known each other for years. I listened to them for a time, but soon grew tired of hearing about their favorite grains and what pastures they liked best. The sky was graying when we finally left the trees behind and the road curved to meet a river. With the ground rising and falling in rock-strewn swells ahead of us, it wasn't until we topped one of the hills that we saw a town nestled in the sweeping curve of the riverbank. A new-looking stone wall stood between it and the river.

"That," said Eadric, "is Chancewold."

"You mean you've been there before?" I asked.

"Once, before I met you. Look, there's Goodman Bentwin now."

The sun was setting as we reached the town and met the crowd that had come to greet us. At Broadnik's suggestion, a small group of men accompanied some of my knights and servants to a site downriver large enough to accommodate all of our tents while the rest of our welcoming party led the way through the narrow streets to the town square.

The air was rich with the smell of roasting meat and the garlands of flowers that draped the fronts of the surrounding buildings. Although the cobblestones had been swept clean, the overlooked feathers and bits of straw proved that the farmers had held their market there, probably that very day. Tables and long benches had been set up in the square, and women wearing their best gowns bustled around bringing platters of food and flagons of ale. The whole place had a festive air as if they were celebrating some sort of holiday. From the way they looked at Eadric, I guessed they were.

I listened as the men greeted him like a long-lost friend while the women smiled and curtseyed. A few maidens actually fluttered their eyelashes at him, something I thought no one really did. Eadric treated them all with equal respect, even calling many of the men by name.

The tables had been set up to form a square with a narrow aisle leading to the center. We took our seats at the head table along with Broadnik and the other local notables. Those townsfolk who weren't serving also went to their benches, where they remained standing, watching Eadric expectantly. I could tell that he hadn't noticed, because his attention was already on the food set before us.

"Eadric," I whispered. He dipped his hands in the water offered by a little boy with damp hair and a missing front tooth.

"Eadric," I said a little more loudly while he dried his hands and eyed a roasted goose on the platter closest to his plate.

"Eadric!" I said again, jabbing him with my elbow as inconspicuously as I could when he leaned across me to reach for the bread.

"What?" he said, nearly dropping it.

"I think they want you to say something," I whispered, nodding toward the townspeople.

"Hmm?" Eadric's mouth was already full. He looked up and saw everyone watching him. Swallowing hastily, he wiped his mouth with the back of his hand and stood. "Good folk of Chancewold, it is wonderful to be back in Upper Montevista among my own people. It is even better that you invited my beloved, Princess Emeralda of Greater Greensward, and myself to eat with you tonight.

Thank you for offering us your gracious hospitality and all of this marvelous food. Now, since I'm sure you are all hungry, and I know I am, let's dispense with any more formality and enjoy this delightful meal!"

While Eadric spoke, the townspeople smiled and nodded, studying me with interest when he called me his beloved and laughing when he said that he was hungry, as if indulging a favorite son or nephew. Apparently, Eadric's habits were as well known in Chancewold as they'd become at my castle.

The meal was a feast with roast poultry and game, a full side of beef, and a stew made of fish cut into chunks in a peppery sauce. Even the vegetables were hotter than I was used to, but only a few things were so spicy that I couldn't eat them.

Eadric, however, ate everything, no matter how hot. He smacked his lips and groaned with pleasure more than once, although he did reach for his flagon of ale to wash down each bite of the fish. We were nearly through the meal when five young couples dressed in brightly colored clothes filed into the center of the square and a musician strummed his first note. A drum and a pipe soon joined in as the couples began to dance. Having nearly eaten his fill, Eadric looked up to watch the dancers whirl past.

"That's marvelous!" I said as a male dancer tossed his partner into the air and caught her.

"It's a traditional folk dance," said Eadric. "Every movement, every color, every note has a special meaning."

"So tell me, what do they mean?" I asked.

Eadric shrugged. "Don't ask me. I never can remember all that stuff."

"They certainly seem to like you here," I said as yet another maiden flashed him a very warm smile.

Eadric shrugged again. "I killed a dragon for them when it came down out of the mountains to eat the farmers' cattle."

"A dragon!" I said, horrified. We'd come to know quite a few dragons, some of whom had become very close friends.

Eadric patted my hand. "That was before I knew how to talk to them. Before I knew any personally."

"You wouldn't kill one now, would you?" I asked, shivering.

"Of course not," he said, giving me a half smile. "I'd have you talk to him until he flew away."

The dancing wasn't the only entertainment we had that night. After the young couples left the square, a score of older men and women took their places and engaged in a contest of high-pitched warbling that they said was the way mountain folk talked to their neighbors. When an older man with a barrel chest won the contest, a tiny red-headed woman came out to demonstrate local birdcalls. She started with a few songbirds, then moved on to the calls of bigger birds such as the eagle, the phoenix, and the roc, the biggest bird of all. Each time she paused to take a breath between roc screeches, we could hear horses screaming in terror just outside the town square. I'm sure I wasn't the only one who was relieved when she sat down.

The tables had been cleared, the last of the ale poured when a maiden with silvery braids (and probably more than a little fairy blood) approached our table and flashed a smug grin at me, then gave Eadric a saucy wink. "When you were here before, Prince Eadric, we had a different sort of contest," she said. "My friends and I were wondering if you'd like to do it again."

"Yes," called a maiden from one of the tables. "Let's have another kissing contest!"

Eadric turned a deep red and his eyes flicked nervously toward me. "I don't think that's such a good idea," he said, and then he very pointedly gazed up at the stars. "Look at that—it's gotten very late. I think it's time we go to our tents. You wanted an early start in the morning, didn't you, Emma?"

"Of course," I said, and then I turned to the girl leaning against the table. "Prince Eadric doesn't need a contest. He already knows who the best kisser is."

"I do indeed," he said, sounding relieved. Taking my hand, he leaned toward me for a kiss. It wasn't long, but it was warm and tender.

The silver-haired girl turned on her heel and flounced off to her seat while the other maidens glared at me.

When Eadric had eaten his last bite and taken his last sip, Broadnik said, "We'll escort you to your tents. Your men have pitched them farther away from the river in a level spot nestled between the hills. We'll have to pass a bend in the river to get to it, so stay close together. It isn't safe by the river at night." Clearing his throat, he glanced at the men seated nearby before turning back to Eadric. "That's something we wanted to talk to you about, but we wanted you to have the chance to enjoy your dinner first. We've been having a problem with sea monsters the last year or so. It's why we built the wall. We were hoping you might be able to help us."

Eadric stood and patted Ferdy, whom he rarely took off anymore. "Don't worry," he said. "A sea monster that could make it this far upriver won't be any problem for my singing sword."

"You have a singing sword?" asked the boy who was missing a tooth. "Can I see it?"

While an admiring crowd of men and boys gathered around Eadric and Ferdy to escort them to the river, I was left to follow with my ladies-in-waiting. Some of the local maidens stayed behind to help clear the square; the rest tagged along as we filed through the streets. From the venomous glances they gave me, I was sure they were hoping that I'd trip and fall into the river headfirst, leaving Eadric available again.

Although enough townsfolk carried torches to fend off the darkness, they couldn't block the night's sounds as we entered the rugged terrain surrounding the town. Unseen birds called warnings at our approach, and deep-throated insects thrummed in the rocks nearby. A howling in the distance was plaintive, with an oddly human quality. Eadric had told me that werewolves plagued his kingdom off and on; they must have come back.

As we passed the end of the wall and drew closer to the river, the rushing water nearly drowned out the cries of the birds, and I could smell the pungent odor of freshwater and dead fish. The women from town who had gone this far left us, some of the torch-bearing men hurrying them back. The rest of the men became more vigilant, breaking off their conversation with Eadric to study the river. I noticed that the men around me were armed with pitchforks and stout sticks, as if they could be of any use against a sea monster.

"The river looks so peaceful," I said to the young man closest to me.

"It looks peaceful because it's deep," he said, holding his torch high. "This is the Yaloo River. Its headwaters are in the mountains north of here. By the time it gets this far, it's very deep and stays that way as far as the sea. You wouldn't believe what we've seen in these waters this past year. Some monsters have started going upriver to spawn, but the real horrors are the ones that come here to eat them. We used to enjoy walking by the river, but now it isn't safe for man nor b—"

Something enormous splashed in the middle of the river, sending wavelets over the bank almost to our feet. Torches were held higher, their light reflecting off the water where ripples continued to arrow in our direction. Whatever was out there was coming our way. Their swords drawn, my knights ran to join Eadric on the riverbank.

"Get back, Your Highness!" said the young man as others hustled me behind an outcropping of rock. I could hear the cries of the ladies-in-waiting as they huddled together close by. The men hovered around me for a moment, but when one of the villagers near the water called out, they ran back to join their companions, shouting, "Stay there!" to me and taking their torches with them. I tried to follow them, only to have the one man who had been left to guard me block my way. Retracing my steps, I strained to hear what was going on while trying to think of how I could help without it being obvious that I was using magic.

I heard running feet, the slap of something large and wet on stone, a man crying out, then Ferdy's familiar voice. "Slash, hack, chop and whack . . . ," he sang, which meant that Eadric was fighting the sea monster.

Hiking up the hem of my gown, I was trying to climb

the rock to see if I could help when there was a high-pitched keening and the rush of wings, and something hit me in the chest, knocking me back the few feet I had climbed. I landed on the ground with an *Oof!* then struggled to sit up, realizing when I couldn't that something heavy was weighing me down and had started to lick my face. My hands met scales when I tried to push it off.

"Emma," said the voice of an adolescent dragon, "I've been looking all over for you. See what I won!"

I rubbed my eyes and tried to see my assailant in the near dark. From the sound of his voice I knew it was my friend Ralf, but I couldn't make out what he was doing. "Ralfie," I said, "you shouldn't be here!"

Ralf backed out of the shadow of the rock and into the moonlight. "I had to come, Emma. I've been looking all over for you and then I heard you were here and I had to show you my award! See," he said, using his claws to hold up a ribbon that dangled from his neck. Some sort of oddly shaped stone hung suspended from the ribbon, twirling in the dim light.

"How did you win it?" I asked, peering at the stone.

"I graduated from dragon geography class with top honors," he said. "We're going to have a big feast to celebrate, and my parents and I want you to come. It's tomorrow night and . . ."

The sea monster roared and it must have been fairly

close, because water splattered down on us from above, drenching us both. Then the sound receded as if the monster were moving off.

"Thank you for inviting me, Ralf, but you shouldn't be here. If those men see you, you'll be in big trouble. Please go back to your parents' cave. I'll come see you as soon as I get home."

"But Emma," Ralf whined, thrashing his tail. "I really want you to come! It won't be the same unless . . ."

"Over here!" someone shouted. "It's a dragon!" I glanced up to see the man who had been guarding me standing only a few yards away, hefting a pitchfork in his hand.

"Ralf," I whispered, "please go!"

"That man has a poky thing, Emma!" said Ralf. "I can't go; he might hurt you! Where's Eadric? Why isn't he here to keep you safe?"

"That man isn't going to hurt me, Ralf, but he will hurt you if you don't go! Please, Ralf, just . . ."

"Back away from it, Your Highness!" shouted the man. "Even the small ones are deadly." Other men had begun to gather behind him, including some of my knights.

Ralf began taking deep breaths to stoke the fire in his belly. He had only recently begun eating gunga beans and hot flami-peppers to get his fire going. Although his flame was feeble compared with what it would be someday, it was enough to injure someone. I didn't have any choice. If I didn't use my magic, someone was bound to get hurt.

The man with the pitchfork was edging around Ralf, with the little dragon turning to face him. "Prince Eadric!" called the townsman. "Here's another dragon for you to kill!"

Eadric shouted, but I couldn't make out his words. It was Ferdy's voice that rang out loud and true above the noise around me.

> Take that, you monster from the deep!
> It's time for your eternal sleep.
> With one more slice and one more whack
> I'll see that you cannot come back!

I shrieked and froze where I was, pretending to be frightened. Holding my hand over my mouth as if I were terrified, I whispered the beginning of a spell.

> Hide this dragon—scale and claw,
> Tooth and fiery breath—

The sea monster roared, and a huge chunk of bloody flesh flew over the boulder and slammed into my legs, sending me sprawling. The rest of the spell I was about to say flew out of my head.

Ralf had built up a good flame. Nearly five feet long, it kept the men from getting too close. Unfortunately, maintaining such a big flame while dodging the jabbing pitchfork made him a little light-headed and confused. By the time I was able to sit up and saw that Ralf had began to fade from sight, he was whimpering and his flame was sputtering.

"That dragon's wearing a magic charm!" shouted another townsman when Ralf had nearly faded away. "Look, he's disappearing!"

"Get him before he's gone altogether!" yelled another voice.

I groaned when I saw that the incomplete spell hadn't been enough. Only parts of the little dragon had disappeared. Everything covered with scales had faded away, which meant that his body, wings, tail and head were gone. His claws were gone, too, as were his teeth and the last of his flame. Unfortunately, his eyes were still visible, as were the pads of his feet and the tip of his nose. His award still dangled from his invisible neck, and when he ran toward me, I could see his damp footprints in the torchlight.

"Ralf," I said under my breath. "Go home!"

"Not until I know you're safe," he told me.

The men rushed me, pushing me away from Ralf so they could form a circle around him. Happy that I'd been forgotten once again, I took the opportunity to whisper a new spell.

Murky fog, come to this place.
Of this dragon leave no trace.
Neither print nor sound nor scale.
Of this dragon leave no trail.

A thick fog rolled in off the river, enveloping everyone and everything. It was a strangely silent fog, absorbing all the sounds Ralf made and some of the men's as well. While the men floundered around, trying to find Ralf without hurting each other, I backed away and called his name. A moment later, the little dragon bumped into me. Nudging me with his nose, he pushed me away from the men. When we had gone far enough that they couldn't hear us, I bent down and wrapped my arms around Ralf's neck.

"You're very brave, Ralf," I said. "Thank you for protecting me."

Ralf may have tried to say something, but the fog still absorbed his voice.

"I need to take the spells off you, but we have to be very quiet. Those men are awfully close. As soon as you're back to normal, you'll have to go home. And don't worry. I'll be fine. No one is going to do anything to me. Understand?" With my arms around him, I could feel the little dragon nod. I said the spell quickly before anyone could interrupt us and was still hugging him when he reappeared.

"Remember, you're going to come see me when you go home again," said Ralf.

"I won't forget," I said.

The little dragon licked my face with his hot, rasping tongue before slipping away into the night. Although I was relieved to see him go, my nerves still jangled. I hated the way doing magic in secret made me feel. When Eadric and I were wed, if he became king of Upper Montevista, I'd be queen of this country. I didn't like the thought of lying to my future subjects, now or ever.

The fog had dissipated into the night, leaving the air cold and clammy. The men soon found me and assumed that I'd wandered off while trying to get away from the dragon. Eadric was with them, having dispatched the sea monster with Ferdy's help, but I could tell that he was not as jubilant about it as he would have been only a few years earlier. Getting to know dragons had made it harder for him to kill monsters, even when he didn't have a choice. Eadric didn't tell me any details other than that he'd be sending some of his men to protect the villagers from passing sea monsters. He did, however, seem concerned about me.

"Are you sure you're all right?" he asked. "The men said you were in real danger."

I patted his arm. "I was fine. Ralf came looking for us, which wouldn't have been a problem if your friends from Chancewold hadn't seen him. He's gone now, but I promised we'd go for a visit as soon as we could." Yawning, I leaned against him and rested my head on his shoulder.

"Let's go find our tents," Eadric said, hugging me to his side. "It's been a very long day."

I was fighting to keep my eyes open when he lifted the flap to my tent. Swaying on my feet, I gazed bleary-eyed through the opening, too tired to take another step. Eadric swung me into his arms and kissed me on the cheek as he carried me inside, setting me on the bed in the corner.

He was straightening up when Hortense stormed into the tent. "Have you no sense of decency?" she hissed at him. "You shouldn't come anywhere near her tent at night. And you!" she said, rounding on me. "You should be ashamed of yourself, letting him in."

"We weren't doing anything," I mumbled sleepily, feeling like a small child.

"That doesn't matter. You two should never be alone in here, especially not at night. Do you know what you're doing to her reputation?" Hortense said, turning back to Eadric.

"But we're getting married as soon as we can arrange it!" said Eadric.

"Hmph!" said Hortense. "As if that mattered! Queen Chartreuse was right to send me. Who knows what you two would be up to if I weren't here!"

Having a lovely kiss good night, I thought as Hortense ushered Eadric out of my tent. Too tired to change into my nightclothes, I stretched out on the bed and fell asleep.

Five

Eadric woke everyone before the sun was fully up the next morning. He said he wanted to get an early start, but I had the feeling that he was afraid the maidens from the town might embarrass him again if we stayed longer.

I was still tired, so I chose to ride in the carriage with Li'l and Shelton. Maybe I'd be able to sleep a little longer.

"Li'l told me about the sea monster," Shelton announced once the carriage was under way.

"I heard the noise and went to investigate," said Li'l. "That thing was big! Eadric was brave to fight it the way he did. When it dragged him into the water, I was sure we'd never see him again, but then he popped up like a cork and climbed out."

I could feel a knot form in my stomach. "Eadric was in the river?"

"For a really long time," she said.

"I wish I'd been there," said Shelton. "I could have

shown him how to fight a sea monster. Remember when the three of us climbed into that sea monster's mouth and . . ."

"I remember," I said, not wanting to think about Eadric facing something like that alone.

No longer sleepy, I signaled for my carriage to stop long enough for me to get out and reach Gwynnie. Eadric was happy to see me and just as tired as I was. We rode together, enjoying each other's company without needing to say a word. After a time I dozed in the saddle, and Eadric may have as well. When my head nodded sharply, waking me with a start, we were in the foothills and could see the snowcapped mountains in the distance.

By noon we'd entered a pine forest so dark that it seemed as if night had fallen. I was wondering how much farther we'd have to go when Eadric said, as if reading my thoughts, "My parents' castle isn't far once we get out of this forest."

"So we'll reach it tonight?" I asked, looking forward to a nice soft bed.

"No, but at the rate we're going, we'll be there tomorrow. We're making really good time. If I didn't know better, I'd say that it was almost magical." Eadric smiled when he said it, but I thought he looked a little wistful.

"It would have been a lot faster if some people had more understanding subjects in their kingdoms," I muttered.

"Isn't it almost time to eat?" Eadric asked, patting his stomach.

I glanced up, but the trees blocked my view of the sky. When I started to look away, something dark darted past at the edge of sight. "What was that?" I asked.

"I didn't see anything," said Eadric.

Another dark shape shot through the trees, squawking. "Did you see that?"

Eadric shrugged. "It was probably just a crow."

"It was too big to be a crow," I said, shaking my head.

And then they were all around us, landing beside the horses like a small noisy flock. If Bright Country hadn't stayed so calm, I'm sure Gwynnie wouldn't have either, but she only snorted and pranced a few paces, letting me calm her with my hand and a few soft words. The knights behind us had a more difficult time with their mounts, who bucked and fought the reins while the carriage horses screamed and tried to rear up.

Although it seemed like more at first, only four witches hopped off their broomsticks, cackling and talking all at once. "Hello there, lovebirds!" called a familiar voice. It was Oculura, the witch who had moved into the old cottage in the enchanted forest near my castle. Her sister, Dyspepsia, was there as well, looking as sour-faced as ever. I'd never seen the other witches before.

"Why don't you introduce us?" said the shorter of the two, a woman with curiously pale skin.

66

"Princess Emeralda, Prince Eadric," said Oculura, "I'd like you to meet my friends Klorine and Ratinki. Klorine is the pushy one." The witch who had asked for an introduction had come forward with her hand extended. It took me a moment to realize that she wanted to shake mine.

"Pleased to meet you," she shouted, pumping my hand up and down until my shoulder ached. "I've heard so much about you two. When we learned that you were going to pass through our woods, I made sure we came out to greet you." I nodded, slightly dumbfounded. Klorine had a very odd way of talking. Not only did she speak loudly, enunciating each word distinctly, but she paused after each sentence as if waiting for someone else to speak, although it was obvious that she hadn't finished what she was going to say.

I waited for her to say something else until she looked at me expectantly and smiled. "Um, yes, well, it's nice to meet you," I said, turning to Eadric for help when the woman wouldn't let go of my hand. He didn't notice, however, because he was squirming under the unyielding gaze of the other witch, Ratinki. Skinny and wrinkled like an old apple, she had to be one of the oldest women I had ever met. With the dirt on her clothes and skin and the odor wafting toward us, she also had to be the smelliest.

"Let go of her hand," said Oculura to Klorine, prying the little witch's fingers from mine. My hand had gone numb, so I shook it while they both looked at me apologetically.

"Sorry," Klorine nearly shouted. "I'm not used to talking to real people. I live in a cave with an echo for company."

"You remember me, of course," said Dyspepsia, looking grumpy. As I'd invited them to visit us at the castle only the week before, I thought it was a very odd question.

"Hello, Dyspepsia," I said. "It's nice to see you again."

Apparently mollified, she grunted and rubbed the small of her back. "Back's paining me again. Broom riding does it every time."

"Got anything to eat around here?" interrupted Klorine.

Eadric perked right up, turning away from Ratinki for the first time since her arrival. He grinned when I said, "I'll see what I can do."

While the servants tended to the horses and the knights stood guard, Eadric and I joined the witches at the base of a tree. I'd invited the ladies-in-waiting to sit with us, but after seeing our guests, Lucy claimed that she'd rather eat our normal travel fare in the shelter of the carriage. Hortense made a point of sitting between me and Ratinki, who spit onto her palm and used the moisture to wash her hands. Although Hortense looked horrified, she didn't say anything to the witch.

We were making ourselves comfortable on the blanket when Ratinki spoke for the first time. In a rough and gravelly voice, she turned to Hortense and said, "I saw the way you looked at me. I'm going to turn you into a slug for that."

Pointing a wavering finger, the old woman said,

> That young woman sitting there
> Didn't have to stop and stare.
> Make her be a slimy slug,
> A slippery, gooey, squishy bug.

"No, wait," I said, throwing up my hand as I recited a quick blocking spell. There was a soft fizzling sound and . . . nothing happened. Hortense continued to sit there looking as prim and proper as always. When it was obvious that she wasn't going to change, I turned to Ratinki and said, "Please don't cast spells on anyone in my party. I need to get them back to my kingdom just as they left it."

"You are good!" the old witch growled. "Oculura said that you were powerful, but I didn't believe her until now. I've never seen anyone block one of my spells before. And that was fast, too!" She scowled and rubbed her mottled scalp under her wispy white hair.

"You'll have to excuse them," said Oculura. "Ratinki and Klorine live deep in the woods and don't talk to people very often."

"Do you live in a cave, too?" I asked Ratinki.

"Wouldn't dream of it!" she exclaimed. "Damp, nasty things! I have a nice little one-room hovel with a good rebuilding spell. Every time the villagers burn it down, it's back three days later, good as new."

Even Eadric looked horrified. "The villagers burn your home?"

Ratinki nodded. "Every few years. I don't mind too much—gets rid of the vermin."

"Why don't you move away?" I asked.

"Why should I? They aren't bad folk. Aside from pelting me with rotten vegetables and setting their dogs on me and stealing my food and . . ."

"Burning your hovel?" Klorine said helpfully.

"Yeah, that, too," said Ratinki. "Aside from those things, they leave me alone and I leave them alone and that's the way it should be. Besides, if I moved away, who would I spy on when I got bored?"

Eadric's stomach rumbled, reminding me of why we were sitting there. The food we'd brought with us was bland and none too plentiful, so after casting a quick searching spell to make sure that no one else from Upper Montevista was around, I pointed at the center of the blanket and said,

Pies and cakes and hot eel stew,
Tarts and breads and berries new.

Bring us lots of tasty food.
We're in a hungry kind of mood.

"Wow!" said Klorine when the food appeared on the blanket. "You can do that? I wish I could! Then I'd never go hungry again!"

"I don't do it very often," I hurried to say when I saw Eadric's expression. He looked as if he'd just won the biggest prize in the biggest tournament. Actually, I'd never made food purely through magic before, so I was a little apprehensive about how it would taste. I needn't have worried.

"This is good!" said Ratinki through a mouthful of fresh bread.

Sampling the eel stew, Klorine exclaimed, "This is better than good! This is the best food I've ever eaten."

"I'm glad you like it," I said, watching Eadric take an entire rhubarb pie.

I sat back, eating very little while enjoying the blissful looks on our guests' faces. I was curious, though—was Ratinki's treatment at the hands of the townspeople typical? When Klorine began to slow down, I asked her, "And how well do you get along with your neighbors?"

"Who, me?" she replied. "Just fine. My closest neighbor is a nymph who lives in the bottom of a lake in my cave. I don't see her very often, but when I do, she's always friendly."

"I meant your nonmagical neighbors."

Klorine shrugged. "None of them lives very close. The ones who come by don't know I'm there."

"You did have that one run-in, though," said Oculura.

"That was years ago. I was young and foolish then. I helped a girl find her soul mate, but he didn't like her when she found him. She was disappointed and told her whole village that I'd ruined her life. They came after me and I had to hide in the woods. That's when I found my cave, so it was a good thing after all. Any more of those tarts? I really like the ones with blueberries."

Even Eadric finished before Klorine and Ratinki, who ate until the very last crumb was gone. When it was time for them to leave, they had eaten so much that they had to struggle to get their brooms off the ground while Oculura and Dyspepsia circled impatiently above them.

I was climbing back into my carriage when Hortense came running over. "I didn't want to say anything in front of those women, but their manners are atrocious. And the stories they tell . . . I shudder to think about it. I hope you aren't going to let yourself be unduly influenced by them. Your mother would never approve if she knew you were keeping company with women like that."

I sighed and paused with my foot on the step. "I'm sure you're right. She doesn't approve of most of the things I do."

I'd started to pull myself into the carriage when Hortense placed her hand on my arm. "That's not all," she said. "I wanted to thank you for what you did back there. Thank you for stopping that horrid woman from . . . from . . ."

"Turning you into a slug?"

"Yes," she said, cringing. "Precisely."

"You're welcome," I said. "Although may I suggest that the next time you encounter someone you find disagreeable you not let it show on your face. I may not always be around to stop them."

Hortense nodded. "Yes," she said, her expression serious. "I'll have to work on that."

It wasn't until we stopped for the night that Eadric and I discussed what the witches had told us. Li'l had already left for her nightly excursion and wouldn't be back until morning. Everyone else except the guards and Hortense had gone to their tents. The senior lady-in-waiting was not about to shirk her duty, and I knew she wouldn't go to bed until I did. With our backs to the fire, Eadric and I shared a large rock while we watched the dancing shapes that the flames cast on the trees around us.

"I didn't know life was so awful for witches here," I said. "Poor Ratinki seems to think that living the way she does is normal."

"I had no idea," said Eadric.

I reached for his hand and squeezed it. "You have to do something. Make some sort of decree or law or something."

Eadric picked up a pebble and chucked it into the woods. "I can when I'm king, but there's not much I can do about it now. Even then I don't know if it would do much good. I can't make people like someone."

"Witches in Greater Greensward are treated with respect, but it's different here. I don't understand why these witches stay in Upper Montevista if they're so obviously hated."

Eadric shrugged. "It's where they've always lived. They don't know that it doesn't have to be this way. Besides, having a Green Witch is why witches are respected in Greater Greensward. You help keep it safe to live there. The witches here don't help at all."

"Why should they? People get angry with them when they try. You heard Klorine. When the girl she helped wasn't happy with the results, she turned on the witch who had helped her."

"Maybe that isn't the kind of help the people of Upper Montevista really need," he said, swatting at a mosquito tickling his cheek.

I opened my mouth to reply, then closed it with a snap. Maybe Eadric was right. Maybe they needed help, but only of a certain kind. I wished there was something I could do about it.

While Eadric and I shared a long and pleasant kiss, Hortense cleared her throat and muttered to herself, letting us know that she disapproved. She was still watching us when we said good night and retired to our tents. I was almost asleep when the werewolves started to howl. They sounded awfully close, certainly close enough to make everyone nervous. I heard the guards talking and the jangle of metal as the men who were supposed to be off duty joined them. Voices from the other tents told me that nearly everyone else was awake as well, although I thought I heard Eadric snoring.

Back home I would have chased away the werewolves long before this, but I'd been so conscious of not upsetting the Upper Montevistans that I'd done nothing, hoping that the creatures would leave us alone. But lying there in the dark, listening to the worried voices of the people around me, I knew that I'd have to take some sort of action or spend the night waiting for the first step of a stealthy paw, the first ragged scream cut short. Slipping out of my tent, I told the closest guard to let the others know that I would take care of it and that they needn't worry. Jumpy people shoot at anything that moves, and a stray arrow in my back was the last thing I needed.

I made my way only a short distance into the woods, then took on the most effective form I knew, the one that had become second nature to me over the last few months—a dragon.

The change was fast now—so fast that it happened between one breath and the next, but with great speed came great pain. When I could breathe again, I was iridescent peridot green with dark emerald claws and pale green translucent wings, more than fifteen feet long and able to breathe fire. Like Ralf's mother, I had acquired a taste for gunga beans and flami-peppers.

Raising my wings above my head, I brought them down in a mighty sweep that brushed the boughs on either side and lifted me above the tops of the trees. I'd been facing the direction of the werewolves' voices, but they'd moved and I moved with them. Dragons can see perfectly well in the dark, and can switch from normal vision to the kind that sees the heat that warm bodies give off. I used both, noting the doe and her twin fawns asleep side by side, the squirrels curled up in their nests, and the paler warmth of the turtle losing the heat it had absorbed during the day.

Wolves were easy to find, but I was hunting werewolves, who were smarter than their nonmagical counterparts and far more malicious. The first time I'd encountered them, I'd hoped that I could talk them into leaving my kingdom, but werewolves are devious and won't listen to logic. I'd had to singe their tails with flame to drive them out then and every time after that. I already knew that I'd have to do the same now.

Following their trail, I circled around toward our camp. I was in no mood for conversation, certainly not with hairy ruffians who liked ripping throats out and would be more than happy to lap the blood of my entourage. With a roar that shook the pine trees until needles rained from the boughs, I swept down on them, breathing a long pinpoint of flame that stopped just short of their furry backs, herding them ahead of me.

I was congratulating myself on a job well done when the pack split in two, leaving me to choose which faction to follow. Picking the smaller group, I tried to herd them back to their fellows, but found that I had to chase each werewolf when they went their separate ways. Because I had no desire to start a fire that could engulf a dry pine forest and knew that flaming too often might do just that, I decided to use a talent other than fire. Twisting and turning between the trees, I flew just above werewolf height, following the biggest beast. Dragons can fly faster than the swiftest horse can gallop, so I had no problem catching up with the werewolf and snatching its tail with my claws. The werewolf writhed in my grasp, snapping and snarling, but it weighed too much to turn back on its own tail and reach me.

Hauling the werewolf into the air, I carried it to the top of the tallest tree and deposited it on one of the sturdier branches. A regular wolf might have squirmed and fallen to its death, but a werewolf possessed human cunning as well as the animal kind. Crying pitifully, the werewolf held on to the swaying branch while I collected its pack-mates one at a time. When I'd gathered the entire pack, I grasped a tail in each of my clawed feet and carried them out of the woods and up the side of a mountain, depositing them on the shores of an isolated island surrounded by near-freezing water before flying back down the mountain for more. If it had been my kingdom, I would have carried them even farther. Since it wasn't, I just wanted them to stay away until we had left their territory.

When I'd moved the last of them, I turned and headed toward our camp. Before landing, however, I checked to make sure that everyone was all right, then flew on, not wanting to stop being a dragon just yet.

There were only two drawbacks to being a dragon. First, it made me feel fearless, and sometimes a little fear was a very good thing. I took risks when I was a dragon that I never would have considered as a human. Second, being a dragon was so much fun, so exciting, so *enticing*, that it was tempting to stay that way a little bit longer each time. My greatest fear, however, was that if I did, I might want to stay that way forever.

Turning back into my human self was particularly difficult that night. Chasing down the werewolves had taken most of the night, making me remain in my dragon form longer than I ever had before. Being a dragon felt so right, so perfect for me that I began to wonder if I really had to go back. Physically I felt wonderful; my blood coursed hotter, my muscles were stronger, I could fill my lungs with one deep breath and hold it for minutes at a time. My reflexes were faster, too, and my mind seemed sharper. And there were so many things that a dragon could do that a human could scarcely imagine. I could fly, swooping low or soaring high, pivoting on a wing tip or gliding for endless miles. I could bathe in lava or burrow through mountains of ice, and all the while feel as comfortable as a human on a warm spring day. A whole world waited to be explored in a way only dragons could manage. If I remained a dragon, I could see sights no human had ever seen, go places no human had ever gone. I'd never have to put up with people like Frazzela or my mother or . . .

And then I thought about my dear, sweet Eadric, who never failed to hold my hand when he thought I might be frightened, who always tried to come between me and danger even when I didn't need him to, and who cared how I felt about nearly everything. Eadric was kind and strong and brave and honorable—the kind of knight that other knights only claimed to be. He was also the love of my life, no matter what form I happened to take.

Although staying a dragon meant that I'd be free to do whatever I wanted to for the rest of my life, I already had something even better waiting for me in a tent, snoring so loudly that I could almost believe I heard him from far away. I could be a dragon now and then, but I knew that I could never leave Eadric for long.

Dipping one wing, I turned around again, heading back to camp and the far more ordinary life of a human witch.

Six

As a dragon I'd seen that we had almost reached the edge of the forest, so I wasn't surprised when the trees thinned out, giving way to a rocky slope. Eadric assured me that his parents' castle was only half a day's ride away. I'd been hoping it would be much closer.

The road we were on wound around the mountainside. Although it afforded us fantastic views, the steep incline tired the horses and made our travel slower. We hadn't gone far beyond the tree line when the ground began to shake and pebbles shifted under the horses' hooves, making them skittish and hard to control.

"Are earthquakes common here?" I asked Eadric.

"Not at all," he said. "I don't think this is an earthquake. Notice how rhythmic it is? I think it's probably a ..."

"Giant!" shouted Lucy, pointing wildly as she hung out of the carriage window. The curve of the mountainside prevented us from seeing more than the giant's head

81

and shoulders, although it was enough to tell that he wasn't in very good shape. His coarse brown hair stuck out from his head like straw, and his tunic was rumpled and dirty, unlike most of the giants I'd seen who kept themselves very well groomed. From the way he was moving he looked as if he were staggering, his head lolling with every step.

"This is bad," said Eadric. "There's a village just a few miles farther in that direction."

"I can't imagine why a giant would want to go so close to a village unless he wants to make trouble," I said. "He has to know how much damage he can do just by walking down the street." A giant this big could do even more damage than most. His head was higher than my father's tallest tower and broader than that of any giant I'd seen before.

"He's either sick or drunk," said Eadric. "Look at the way he's walking. I'll go see which it is. You stay here with the carriages, Emma. It's safer here. There's no telling what he'll do when he sees me."

"Then you shouldn't go by yourself," I said, turning Gwynnie to join him. "I can use my magic to stop him if he's really out of control."

Eadric looked exasperated when he shook his head and said, "If you won't stay here because I ask you to, consider how many people there are in the village who could see your magic. Do you really want to risk it?"

"But . . . ," I began, then realized that he was right.

Unlike Greater Greensward, where my father's subjects expected me to confront trouble, the people of Upper Montevista would be horrified to see a princess facing a giant and even more so when they realized that I was a witch.

I watched helplessly from Gwynnie's back as Eadric and my knights picked their way across the rocky ground. "I can't just sit here," I muttered to myself. After what had happened with the sea monster, I wasn't about to let Eadric face the giant without me. Biting my lip, I tried to decide what to do. Without any trees or shrubs to hide behind, I couldn't very well change without anyone seeing me, unless . . .

I was all fumble fingers as I tied Gwynnie behind my carriage, although the mare was the only one to notice. Li'l was asleep, hanging upside down from the carriage roof. Shelton, however, was wide awake, clutching the window frame and waving his eyestalks with excitement as he watched the giant's progress.

"Is that a real person?" he asked as I swung the door open and climbed in. "He's ever so much bigger than you."

"He's a giant," I said. "They're all bigger than me. He isn't acting right, so I'm going to go see why."

"But I heard Eadric," said Shelton. "He said you should stay here. I admit he's a bossy know-it-all, but I think he's right this time. If that giant is real, no one should go near him, least of all you. What would happen to me if something happened to you? Eadric would probably cook me or feed me to some wild beast."

"Thanks for being so caring," I said. "I'll be fine and so will you. Now stand back."

It took only a moment for me to turn into a hawk. Not only was the bird fast, but it had marvelous eyesight, and right now that was what I needed most. I didn't dare get too close since I didn't want to be seen, so I'd have to watch from a distance. Springing from the carriage window, I took to the air, spiraling upward until I had almost reached the high, puffy clouds. I glanced down and saw Eadric and the knights approaching the giant, who was only a few strides from the outermost building in the village. He looked drunk to me, and I was certain of it when I heard him start to sing.

> Oh, give me an ale, a stout-hearted ale
> In a bottomless, endless mug.
> I'll do my best to drain it dry.
> You know I'll give it a good try.
> And if I can't, I'll be coming back
> To try it again tomorrow.

The giant ended his song with a hiccup that shook the village and crumbled chimneys. Looking as if his eyes couldn't quite focus, he was about to set his foot on a wagon loaded with firewood when Eadric and his knights arrived. "Ho there, Giant!" Eadric called. The giant turned, staggering. Closing one eye, he peered down at Eadric and Bright Country.

"Look!" the giant said with a foolish grin on his face. "A puppy!" Reaching for Eadric, he tripped over his own feet and landed on his knees, shaking the ground so that the carriages rattled. "Ouch!" he said. "That wasn't very nice. Bad puppy!"

"This way, Giant," Eadric shouted as the giant crawled to his feet with difficulty, shaking his head and moaning. Spinning Bright Country around, Eadric kicked him into a gallop, taking the rocky terrain far too fast. The other knights ran with him, but the giant seemed interested only in Eadric and the silver-maned Bright Country.

"Come back here, puppy," he shouted loudly enough to start rockslides on the next mountain over. Lurching after Brighty, he followed Eadric away from the village and far across the rock-strewn slope. Although I'd been sure that the destrier would outrun him, the giant was catching up. Eadric must have heard him, because he began turning Brighty in a zigzag pattern, but even that didn't slow the giant.

It was time that someone did something, and that someone was going to have to be me. The giant had given me the idea himself. Because witches' magic doesn't have much effect on beings that exist through magic, I couldn't cast a spell on him. I'd have to cast it on something else without using obvious magic. Pointing a claw at the ground between Eadric and the giant, I said,

> Move the rocks to form a bump—
> Not too high, more like a hump.
> All we want the bump to do
> Is catch the giant by his shoe.

Eadric was still racing away when the ridge rose up, tripping the giant. I held my breath until the giant hit the ground with a splat so loud that Bright Country was blown over and avalanches started on every mountain in the chain. The knights cheered when the giant didn't get up. I began to breathe again when Eadric stood and stepped aside so Bright Country could scramble to his hooves.

When the giant continued to lie there unmoving, I wondered if he'd been injured in his fall. Then, with a snort and a gargle, he began to snore, and I knew that he'd done just what he was supposed to do. The giant had fallen down, and fallen asleep.

I flew back to my carriage when a group of exultant villagers threw open their doors and hurried out to thank Eadric. By the time he returned, I was waiting impatiently astride Gwynnie. "How did it go?" I asked.

"Very well," he said, wiping the sweat from his brow. "I had the giant follow me until he collapsed, exhausted.

I told the villagers to make a lot of noise when he wakes up. That should drive him away."

"Why would noise drive him away?" I asked.

"Because he's going to have a very bad headache when he wakes, and loud noise will only make it worse. He'll leave, all right, as quietly as he can."

"It sounds like you thought of everything," I said.

"I try," Eadric replied, looking very pleased with himself.

I didn't mind that Eadric believed he'd taken care of the giant on his own. He'd been very brave to lead the giant from the village the way he did, and if anyone deserved the credit it was Eadric. However, having to be secretive bothered me enough to put me in a bad mood, which hadn't improved by the time we finally saw the royal castle of Upper Montevista.

It was a forbidding-looking castle, not airy and light like my home. Thick-walled, with few windows and four dull gray towers, it was perched on a jagged pinnacle of rock called Castle Peak with only one route to its gate across a narrow, steep-sided ridge. Although it commanded breathtaking views of the valley far below and much of the mountainside, the castle itself wasn't at all pretty. At least Eadric was happy to see it.

I sat up straighter in my saddle, sorry that I hadn't taken the time to fix my hair and change into a clean gown. The castle guards had already spotted us, and we could see the flurry of activity on the walls. Their prince was coming home.

At Eadric's command, the knights who'd been in front fell back, and the two of us led the way across the ridge. With the ground falling in sheer drops on either side of the road, I could see that the castle would be easy to defend. A drawbridge before the castle gate made unwanted visitors even less likely. As our horses clattered across the wood and we entered the passageway beyond the portcullis, I looked up to see the murder hole from which defenders could drop boulders or pour boiling oil from above. I was glad that we were welcome.

Eadric's parents must have been alerted to our arrival, because they were waiting for us as we entered the courtyard. It was obvious that his mother was upset. Her eyes were red, her face mottled and tear-streaked. Eadric's normally amiable father, King Bodamin, looked angry and very, very worried. At first I thought it was because I was there, but then the queen rushed to Eadric's side, exclaiming, "My darling boy! You've come just when we need you most!"

"Indeed," said his father. "Tell me, son, did you see anything unusual on your way here?"

Eadric and I exchanged glances. "Well," he began. "There was a drunken giant . . ."

Queen Frazzela glanced at the king. "You don't suppose that giant was involved?"

The king shook his head. "I don't know what to think."

"What's going on?" asked Eadric, frowning. "What aren't you telling me?"

The queen sighed and dabbed at fresh tears. "Your brother has been kidnapped."

Her husband looked annoyed. "Now, we don't know that, my dear," he said before turning to Eadric. "The scamp has been ill and tucked in his bed for the past week. Last night he became restive and sneaked out of the castle, something I strongly discourage, I might add. He's been looking for dragon eggs, and he may have thought he'd have better luck at night. Bradston is only ten years old! He knows I don't approve of his solitary forays even when he's healthy, as I've told him . . ."

"Bodamin, you're rambling!" said the queen.

"Ahem, well, yes, I suppose I am. As I was saying, he sneaked out, but wasn't missed for hours because we thought he was in his bed. A stable boy admits to having seen him go. Everyone has been looking for him, except no one can find hide or hair of the rascal. I was afraid that he might have taken a bad fall, so my men have been searching the cliffs and er . . . rocks below."

"He wouldn't have fallen," said Eadric, shaking his head. "Bradston is more agile than a mountain goat. I've never seen him miss a step."

"That's what I said!" wailed the queen. "I know he's

89

still alive, because the banshee hasn't come to tell us that he isn't. And I would have sensed it if my little darling were hurt." A lady-in-waiting offered her a clean cloth to wipe her eyes. The queen took it, handing the woman her soggy one in return as new tears dripped down her pale cheeks. "I just wish I knew where he was. He's still not well and I'm sure he must be terrified."

Eadric looked grim. "Bradston isn't afraid of anything, although he'll have reason to be when I get through with him if this is another of his tricks. Mother," he said, reaching for my hand, "I've brought Emma for a visit. I'd appreciate it if you'd welcome her and make her comfortable while I organize a search party. I'll find Bradston for you."

Queen Frazzela looked at me as if she hadn't realized that I was there, although she couldn't have missed seeing me sitting on my palfrey right next to Eadric. "Ah," she said. "You brought *her*. I suppose it can't be helped, but this is a very bad time to have a visitor, especially one with her inclinations."

"Mother," said Eadric, with iron in his voice. "You can't talk about Emma that way. I want you to remember that this is the girl I'm going to marry. And you can hardly blame her for coming at a bad time. We had no way of knowing about Bradston."

"*She* might have," his mother said with obvious distaste. "You forget that I've seen her true nature. Go, organize your search party. I'll see that the girl is suitably housed." The queen turned to gesture to one of her waiting servants.

"Suitably housed for a princess, you mean," said Eadric.

The queen's back stiffened. "For a princess," she added, although I could tell from her voice that it pained her to say it.

After Eadric took my knights to confer with his father's, I had to wait in the courtyard for someone to show me to my room while Lucy fussed over me. After she'd tidied my hair and straightened my gown, I'd had enough. "You can help me more by seeing to our rooms," I said, trying to shoo her into the castle. Although she went easily enough, Hortense refused to go until I told her that I was exhausted and was relying on her to find a place for me to rest. Satisfied that she had an even greater mission than to wait with me, Hortense bustled off into the castle, determined to set things right.

I was finally free to find my friends. Slipping into my carriage, I fetched a sleepy little bat and a skittery crab, tucking them into my sleeves. Because there was still no sign of anyone coming to get me, I sat down on a step to wait. "Why did the queen leave you out here?" Shelton asked, his voice muffled by fabric. "Coral would never be so rude. Why don't we just go in and have a look around?"

"Because that wouldn't be polite either. As my old nurse used to say, 'Two wrongs don't make a right.'"

Shelton giggled, tickling my arm with his eyestalks. "And two rights don't make a left. That would take three, wouldn't it?"

I laughed for the first time in days, and said into my sleeve, "That's true. I hadn't thought of that."

"Pardon me, Your Highness, are you all right?" someone asked from the steps behind me.

I turned, holding my sleeve to keep Shelton inside. A scullery maid stood at the top of the steps smelling of fresh baked bread.

"I'm fine," I said. "Why do you ask?"

Giving my sleeve a funny look, she curtseyed and said, "No reason. The queen says I'm to take you to your room. Come this way, if you please." I hurried to keep up with the little maid as she took me through a door and up a winding set of stairs. "I can't take long because Cook doesn't know I'm gone and won't be happy if I'm not there to turn the spit." We turned down a corridor lit only by a few narrow arrow slits. "Ah, here we are. It isn't much, but it's better than some. Now, I'd best be off or Cook'll box my ears again."

The maid shut the door behind her, leaving me in a small room with a tiny unglazed window and a pallet on the floor. When I saw that the trunk that stood in one corner was filled with someone else's clothes, I wondered who had been made to give up her room for me.

"Is she gone?" Shelton asked.

"She's gone," I said, pulling him out of my sleeve and setting him on the trunk.

The crab scuttled across the wooden surface, waving his claws in the air. "So this is where they put us? This is disgraceful! It looks like a closet. Even the butler has a better room in Coral's palace. I would, too, if I had a room."

"We'll be fine here," I said, setting Li'l on the trunk beside Shelton. The little bat fell over, murmuring something about drafty caves, and went back to sleep.

The room was dark, depressing, and as drafty as the rest of the castle, but at least it was clean. I didn't think anyone, including the room's usual occupant, would mind if I made it a bit more pleasant. Using some simple spells, I added a bright-colored tapestry to the wall to keep out the draft and turned the pallet into a regular bed, adding feather pillows and a warm blanket. The rest would have to do.

Shelton was trying to peek inside the trunk when I lifted the chain from around my neck and held my farseeing ball to the light coming through the window, saying,

Find the prince who lives here, too.
Find Eadric's younger brother.

Show me where he is right now
Despite his nasty mother.

"You're going to help that awful woman?" asked Shelton, waving his eyestalks at me. "I know I wouldn't if I were you."

"If you were me, we wouldn't be here," I said. "And just because his mother was rude to me doesn't mean that I won't help find the boy. I'm doing this for Eadric, not for her."

I had to wait a while for the spell to work, which surprised me because my magic is usually much faster than that. When an image finally began to appear in the farseeing ball, it was dim, with lights flickering at the edges, and I had to concentrate before I could understand what I was seeing. It was a narrow, stone-walled passage embedded with some kind of shiny pebbles and . . . The passage seemed to move as I watched, but it wasn't the walls that were moving, it was the prince. Striding along as if he owned the place, Bradston was following some sort of creature carrying a torch that . . . I squinted at the farseeing ball. It was a four-headed troll, which meant that, in the troll world, it was a being to be reckoned with. Other trolls followed behind the prince, one with two heads, the rest with only one.

I was peering at the ball, trying to make out where they might be, when the troll in the lead stopped abruptly. One of the heads glanced down; suddenly my perspective changed and all four heads were looking directly at me. Startled, I nearly let go of the farseeing ball.

"I know what you doing," croaked a head with a bad overbite and fiery red hair that had been chopped into short spikes.

"You not do that here," a brunette head spat at me.

My hand shook. I'd never heard voices or any kind of sound from my farseeing ball before. Every time I'd used it, the ball had shown me an image and nothing more. Even worse was the fact that the troll could see me, too. Some new magic was being worked here, and not through anything that I had done. I looked more closely, hoping to get a clue about what was going on. The troll was wearing an ornate golden chain around all four of her necks and was looking into something connected to the chain. From the way she was holding it I wondered if she might have a kind of farseeing ball of her own. But that didn't make sense. Only magic users could see into farseeing balls, yet I'd never heard of a troll having magic.

"You try use magic here, I kill boy in worst way," said the red-haired head. "Go now, unless want me show what can do."

A wavering light approached the troll from behind, resolving into a one-headed troll carrying another torch. "Your Majesties," he said, bowing. "Cave behind treasure room ready."

The four-headed troll whipped around to face him. All of the heads shouted at once, but one head seemed the loudest. "Quiet, numbskull!" she shrilled. "Not now! Can not see I . . ." The image in my farseeing ball went fuzzy, then disappeared altogether, something that had never happened before. I frowned and shook the ball, but no other picture appeared. Sighing, I slipped the farseeing ball back under my neckline. At least I knew what had happened to him and where he had gone. The queen of the trolls had kidnapped Prince Bradston and taken him to her underground home.

"I'll be right back," I told Shelton on my way out the door.

The little crab darted to the edge of the trunk. "Where are you going?" he asked.

"To find Eadric," I said. "I have to tell him what I learned."

Armed with my newfound knowledge, I went in search of Eadric. It didn't take long to find him with a discreet tracer spell, but I had to wait outside the door until he'd finished talking to the assembled knights.

"I know who took Bradston," I said as the last knight left the room. "The troll queen has him."

Eadric rubbed his chin, frowning. "The troll queen, huh? I was sure you were going to say that Jorge and Olebald took him."

"How do you know where Bradston is?" asked

Queen Frazzela. She'd been standing in the corner, and I hadn't seen her when I'd come in.

"I'm sorry you don't like magic, but it was the only way I knew of to find Bradston."

The woman's face turned crimson, and her voice shook as she said, "I knew you would do magic here. You witches are all alike—coming where you aren't wanted to ply your wicked trade. Well, I won't have you casting spells in my castle! I forbid it, do you understand?"

"You forbid it at the cost of your younger son's safety?" I asked, my own voice as steady as I could make it. "Do you really hate magic that much?"

"I . . ." I could tell that the woman had a scathing retort on her lips, but then she seemed to deflate as her maternal side won out. In half-strangled tones she asked, "Where is he? Is he all right?"

"He looked fine, for now. He's in an underground tunnel, wherever the queen makes her home." Turning to Eadric, I asked, "Are there any mines around here? Somewhere you might find precious gems?"

Eadric frowned as he thought. "I remember hearing rumors about Roc Mountain. . . . But that's all they are—rumors. No one who has gone there has ever come back."

"They wouldn't if the trolls lived there, would they? See what you can find out about that mountain. I think that's where we'll find him."

"What do you mean *we*?" demanded Queen Frazzela.

"Who do you think you are to invite yourself along? Eadric will lead the search party, and they won't need you or your horrid magic!"

"I'll have to go with them if either of your sons is to come back. Eadric is the bravest man I've ever known, but even he is no match for a mountain full of trolls. Just who do you think would have the advantage in the queen's own mountain? He won't have a chance without me, so I'm going whether you want me to or not!"

Eadric put his arm around me and pulled me closer to kiss my cheek. "I'd rather you stayed here," he whispered in my ear. "Trolls are horrible creatures, and I may not be able to protect you the way I'd like."

"I'm going with you, Eadric. Don't you know me well enough to know that I can protect myself?"

"With my help," he said. "But I'll be busy helping Bradston."

"And so will I," I said, looking into his eyes so he'd know that I meant it.

Eadric sighed and turned back to his mother. "Emma is the Green Witch—the most powerful witch in her kingdom and probably in ours as well. I'd rather not take her into danger, but if she's willing to go, we stand a much better chance of getting Bradston out safe and sound."

"I see you're siding with her!" the queen said, looking as if she'd been slapped.

"It's not a matter of taking sides. I love Emma,

Mother. I'm marrying her, with or without your permission, and I believe she's right about this."

Queen Frazzela drew herself up to her full height, which was still shorter than either of us. "Just bring Bradston back," she said, her eyes blazing. "And keep your nasty little witch and her horrid magic away from me!"

And this woman is going to be my mother-in-law? I thought, then bit my lip as I wondered how I'd ever be able to spend part of each year living in a castle with her.

Seven

The rest of the day was spent preparing for our expedition. Gathering food and weapons takes time, as does readying horses and men. Later I was told it was amazing that everything was ready to go so quickly. I didn't use any magic where anyone could notice, but if swords were sharpened more easily and food was more plentiful than expected just because I happened to be around, no one seemed to mind. If we had to take an army with us, I wanted to make sure that it didn't hold us back.

Hortense was upset that I was going, but not enough to want to join us. Once Queen Frazzela understood that I was going no matter what, she ignored me until we were about to leave. After a tearful good-bye to Eadric, she turned to me and said, "Take good care of my boys." It wasn't much, but at least it was something.

We were riding through the ranks of soldiers that were waiting to follow us when I noticed the way that some of them were looking at me. As far as I knew I had done nothing to warrant it, but their eyes showed how little they liked me. It made me wonder if they had seen me at the tournament or had simply heard rumors about me. Either way, it left me feeling unsettled and edgy.

The sun was rising over the mountaintop when we crossed the narrow causeway. Because we had to move as quickly and silently as possible, I'd left my carriage behind and rode Gwynnie, who was under strict instructions to be quiet. Both Li'l and Shelton were in my sleeve again, partly because they wanted to go and partly because I didn't want to leave them with Eadric's mother. Although King Bodamin had wanted to accompany us, his leg had swollen with gout and he wasn't in any condition to ride. I felt sorry for him because he was obviously in pain, but pleased that it meant Eadric and I could ride together.

We had scarcely left the causeway when Eadric's second-in-command rode his horse up to ours. "I suggest we take the northern route off the mountain," he said, opening a map drawn on a square of hide. "The trail is steeper, but it would take us to the valley only a few miles from Griffin Pass. There shouldn't be any griffins there this time of year, and it leads east to the foot of Roc Mountain."

Eadric traced the pass with his finger. "That route would add nearly a day to the ride. Wouldn't it be better to approach the mountain from the south?"

"I'd advise against it, Your Highness. A basilisk has moved into these caves," the soldier said, tapping the map. "And there are rumors of other beasts killing travelers here and here. No one has passed that way successfully in two or three years. Whatever is there isn't letting anyone through. And as for the woods beyond . . ."

"We'll take the northern route then," said Eadric. "If we ride harder and faster, we should be able to cut back on any extra time it would take."

"Very good, Your Highness," said his officer, letting his mount drop back as we rode on.

He had been right about the trail being steeper. Eadric and I spoke in muted voices until we reached an area where the slope was angled too sharply for all but the most sure-footed of horses. The trail changed at that point, snaking across the slope, then switching back on itself in a slightly less perilous descent. A small group of soldiers preceded us down the trail while the rest followed behind. We grew quiet, talking only to our horses to reassure them when they balked at the more difficult spots. As we zigzagged across the mountain's face, we could hear the men behind us, out of sight behind the rocks and the spindly trees that grew on that part of the mountain. Gwynnie was nervous, so I still had to give her most of my attention, but I did catch a few words here and there.

". . . a witch, I tell you."

"Where I come from, we drive witches out."

"... might not be true ...

"... hear the queen?"

"... after that tournament ..."

Although I tried not to let their conversation bother me, I couldn't help but remember the way some of them had looked at me in the courtyard. Back home in Greater Greensward I was respected more for being the Green Witch than I'd been for being a princess. Here I had the feeling that being a princess was the only thing that kept them from throwing stones at me. When I turned to say something to Eadric, his jaw was set and he looked angry. It seemed he had heard them, too.

When our horses were on more normal footing again, I tried to distract Eadric by telling him what had happened when I saw the troll queen. We talked about trolls, sharing what we knew. I'd heard that they liked to brag. He'd heard that they were vicious fighters who ate their defeated enemies. We'd both heard that they weren't very smart and that they avoided sunlight, preferring to live in caves and deep forests. It was rumored that the touch of sunlight on their skin could turn them to stone, but neither of us knew anyone who had actually seen that happen. Neither of us knew much about the troll queen either, other than what I'd seen. As we entered another section of the pine forest, we grew silent, not sure who or what might be listening.

We stopped that night in a valley, setting up camp on

both sides of a brush-lined brook that was fed from snow-chilled mountain streams. We were traveling light, so the men were going to sleep out in the open on one side of the brook near the tethered horses. Eadric insisted that I have a tent set up on the far side. I think he was remembering what he'd overheard as well as the way his men had looked at me the few times we'd stopped, because he wouldn't let any of them come near me.

I went to bed as soon as the tent was ready, but the thin fabric didn't prevent me from hearing the cries of unfamiliar birds and night-hunting animals, as well as other creatures that I didn't normally notice. My hearing was still sensitive from the spell I'd used to talk to the butterfly. I hadn't undone it yet because I wasn't sure that I wanted to; I could hear so many interesting things now. But as I lay awake, listening to the mice in the ground under my tent and the aphids on the leaves nearby, and a lot of other creatures that I couldn't identify, I wondered if I might not be better off without it. At least then I might be able to get some sleep.

Suddenly I heard the *whump* of huge wings cutting through the night sky. When the horses started screaming, and I heard the distinctive screech of a griffin, I couldn't just lie there and do nothing. Knowing that griffins were very territorial and wouldn't be able to resist the cry of another of their kind, I sat up in the dark and said a simple spell to have a griffin distress call lead the approaching griffin far into the forest. It was something that *could* have happened on its own, so it shouldn't raise anyone's suspicions.

When I heard the call of the false griffin, its strident notes sounded all too close. As the real griffin responded, the call moved away, leading the griffin farther and farther from our camp. It took a while for the horses to settle down, but when they did, I finally drifted off to sleep . . . and woke up soon after as Li'l popped back into the tent, making the smallest of sounds. After spending most of the day cramped and stiff inside my sleeve, she had gone off to explore when it grew dark. I was surprised that she was back so soon.

"*Psst*, Emma!" she said. "Wake up!"

"Li'l," I said. "It's the middle of the night! What are you . . ."

"Shh! Don't talk, just listen!"

I did then, waiting for her to explain, but it wasn't her voice that she wanted me to hear. Someone or something was coming through the woods and trying to be quiet about it. I listened harder. Whatever they were, there was more than one out there. I tried to shut out the other sounds and focus on the new arrivals. There were a lot of them, and they were coming our way.

"Who are they?" I whispered.

"I don't know," said Li'l. "They're big and ugly and smell bad, and you wouldn't believe it, but some have more than one head and . . ."

"Trolls!" I said, throwing off my blanket. Grabbing Shelton, my shoes, and my cloak, I slipped under the tent flap and would have stumbled over Eadric if there hadn't been a full moon that night to light up the clearing. He was sleeping on the ground in front of my tent, his hand on Ferdy's scabbard. Knowing him, he was probably there to guard me. I clapped my hand over his mouth and shook him by the shoulder. "Eadric, be very quiet and listen to me," I said when his breathing changed and I could tell that he was awake. "Trolls are coming through the woods. We have to warn the others."

I could feel Eadric nod under my hand. "Stay behind me," he whispered when I'd uncovered his mouth. After he'd belted Ferdy's scabbard on his hip, Eadric and I crept toward the brook. We had nearly reached the water's edge when the first troll appeared, bringing with him the smell of rotten eggs. Crouching behind a shrub, we watched as he swung his club in an arc and smashed my tent flat. The ground beneath us vibrated as the troll raised his club over and over again, beating the tent into the soil.

Eadric set his hand on Ferdy and was about to draw him from the scabbard when other trolls appeared, no longer making any effort to be quiet. The smell grew stronger the closer they came, until it was almost over-whelming. I placed my hand on Eadric's to prevent him from waking his sword, then pushed him farther into the brush while the trolls milled around, bellowing so loudly that it hurt my ears.

As other trolls converged on my campsite, I won-dered why they had attacked my tent first and seemed to be ignoring Eadric's men. It was only after they began crashing around that the knights and soldiers had no-ticed them, taking up their weapons before the trolls had even looked their way. The first trolls to see the men now jumped from stone to stone to cross the water, and the fighting began. Men shouted, trolls bellowed, horses screamed while swords flashed in the light of the camp-fires, and clubs thudded against fragile bones. Roaring so loudly that my heart jumped in my chest, the trolls ripped up saplings and used them to knock men flying into the night air, only to land in silent, broken heaps. It was ob-vious that the men were outmatched. One man fell for every swing of a troll's club, yet the men's swords seemed to have little effect on the trolls.

As more trolls entered the clearing, trampling the re-mains of my tent into the dirt, we could hear others com-ing through the woods behind us. Eadric and I were still crouched behind the shrubs when Li'l came back. "You wouldn't believe how many are out there!" she said, flutter-ing her wings in agitation. "The woods are full of them!"

"Your men don't stand a chance!" I whispered to Eadric.

"I have to go help them," he said, trying to pull Ferdy out as he rose from a crouch.

I pulled him back down, saying, "No, you don't. Even Ferdy would be useless in a fight like that. If you go now, you'll be killed. Then where would I be without my Eadric? And what would your brother do without you there to rescue him? Look, your men are retreating."

Eadric looked over in time to see his men leaping onto their horses' backs and tearing up the slope, away from the trolls and us. Instead of following, the trolls lumbered back to the water's edge. "What we do now, Headbonker?" hollered one.

"Follow them, idiots!" shouted a troll with two heads sprouting from his stocky body. He was dressed in a tunic edged with silver and seemed to have an air of authority about him. Gesturing to the rest of his army, he shouted, "All you trolls, hunt humans down!"

"That's not good," I said. "We can't have all these trolls marching on the castle. If I can just keep the other trolls from crossing the . . . I know what I'll do. Keep your head down and Ferdy in his scabbard so I can concentrate."

"What do you have in mind?" Eadric asked.

"You'll see," I said, and began my spell.

This brook sleeps in its graveled bed
As it has since ages past.
Please wake it now and make it grow
To a river deep and vast.

Even in the moonlight I could see the brook changing. Once a yards-wide flow of water only a foot deep,
the brook swelled, overflowing its banks as if flood-
waters from upstream were just now reaching it. The water that had been so clean when we'd stopped for the
night became murky with silt and the plant life it carried
away. It reached the brush where Eadric and I were hiding, forcing us out into the open, but the trolls had gathered by the water and were too intent on what it was
doing to notice us.

The trolls who had been midstream when the water
swelled were swept off their stepping-stones and carried
away, splashing and choking. Those who had been about
to cross turned around and began shoving the trolls behind them. A brawl broke out as the river rose around
their ankles, then up to their knees.

I was wondering what I should do next when I saw
the troll leader coming our way. For the first time I noticed a chain with a ball around his neck that reminded
me of the one I'd seen on the troll queen. "Quiet!" he
bellowed, and the fighting trolls froze in place. While one

head stared at the ball, telling the other head what it saw, the second head looked around as if trying to find whatever the first head was describing. The troll took another step, then another, until the second head glanced our way and saw Eadric and me crouched behind a too-small rock. "She there!" the troll roared, raising his arm to point. The gathered trolls turned to gape. Brandishing their clubs and shouting, the closest ones started lumbering toward me.

As the trolls drew nearer, a dozen spells flew through my mind; I rejected them one after another. I almost turned us into bats, but there was Shelton to consider. Still in my pocket, the little crab wouldn't know how to fly and might be too confused to learn quickly enough. I rejected other animal forms as well, then decided to try a spell I'd never used before. The advancing trolls were only a few club-lengths away when I blurted an invisibility spell. We disappeared a moment later.

The troll closest to us was slow to notice and swung his club anyway, narrowly missing us as Eadric dragged me aside. "Hunh!" the troll grunted when his club thumped the ground. "Where they go?" Raising his club, he examined the underside as if expecting to see us impaled on its pointy spikes. When he saw that we weren't there, he turned to the troll behind him and asked, "Humans get past you, Nortle?"

"Not me!" said the other troll. "Maybe Flart."

"Not past me!" said a shaggy-headed troll with pro-truding teeth. Flart poked the other troll in the stomach with his club. Nortle responded with a gentle tap to Flart's skull.

While the trolls passed the blame for our disappear-ance, Eadric and I tried to slip away, but the poking and tapping quickly turned into fighting, and Eadric and I were caught in the middle where flailing clubs whistled past our heads. When a troll fell against us, Shelton scut-tled out of my sleeve and pulled his hair, hard. The troll yelped and looked wildly around. Shelton lost his balance and was about to fall from my sleeve when I let go of Eadric's hand to grab the little crab. As long as Eadric and I were in contact we could see each other, but the moment I let go, he was as invisible to me as he was to everyone else.

"Eadric!" I whispered loudly, reaching out for him.

"I'm right here," he said, but I held my breath until our probing hands found each other again.

The fighting had spread to the rest of the army. Careful to hold on to each other, Eadric and I crept away while the two-headed leader tried to pull a pile of his sol-diers off each other. When we were safely past the last of the trolls, Eadric helped me climb onto a large flat-topped rock that projected into the current. We stood side by side, gazing back upriver to where the soldiers had camped. The site was abandoned except for a pair of trolls who were pacing back and forth, demanding that their friends come get them, and threatening them if they didn't.

"My men took the horses, so they should be able to outrun the trolls," said Eadric. "They'll be safe once they reach the castle. I want you to go back to the castle now. The quickest way would probably be for you to turn yourself into a bird and fly there. You can stay invisible until you're safely inside."

"I'm not leaving you! You can't be serious if you think I'm going to let you go all the way to Roc Mountain by yourself."

Eadric set his hands on my shoulders and met my eyes with his. "You're not going with me. You mean too much to me to risk taking you there. This expedition has gotten too dangerous, and it's only just begun."

I took half a step back, stopping only because I'd reached the edge of the rock. "Is this what you think our marriage is going to be like? You'll make all the major decisions and tell me what to do? Grassina and Haywood have made all their decisions together for the past few months, and they weren't even married yet. I thought married people were partners who helped each other. If we're going to get married, you'll have to understand that I love you and I'll never let you walk into danger alone. I want you to be safe just as much as you want me to be. I'm going to help you in any way I can, and if that means going into a troll mountain, so be it. Now, you know that we don't have time to argue about this. Bradston needs us as soon as we can get there. This may not be the way you'd originally planned, but we're still Bradston's only hope."

"You can be so stubborn!"

"Only when I have to be," I said. "Like when someone is trying to make me do something that I know is wrong."

Eadric sighed and shook his head. "Then I guess we'd better get started." He held my hand while he hopped off the rock, then helped me down after him. "So," he said as we started to walk, "do you have any idea how that troll with the two heads was able to find us?"

"I think that ball he wore could show him where I'd worked magic. He used it to find us after I changed the brook into a river, and again when I made us invisible. It was probably how he found us in the first place. He must have known where I was by the magic I used in my tent."

"What magic was that?"

"I lured a griffin away from camp. It wasn't a very big spell, but I guess it doesn't have to be for that ball to pick it up. I think it must be a magic-seeing ball. I've heard about them, although there aren't very many around. They're generally made to keep an eye on a troublesome witch or wizard. A farseeing ball can locate just about anyone, but the person who uses it has to have some ability with magic. Magic-seeing balls are different. Although a magic user has to make it, anyone can use it, even someone who has no magic of his own. It locates the witch it was meant to find as soon as she uses her magic. I wondered how the troll queen could see me. It makes sense if she had a magic-seeing ball that was focused on me. Do you suppose the two-headed troll was using the queen's or had one of his own?"

"Let me see if I understand this," said Eadric. "Someone who has no magic can look into that ball and see someone using magic? Does that mean that every time you use magic, that ball is going to tell the trolls where you are?"

"Or at least where I was when I used the magic. I guess I won't be able to say any spells for a while if we don't want the trolls to find us. It will be a lot easier to rescue Bradston if their army doesn't know where we are." I rubbed my temples, trying to massage away the headache that was just beginning. "There's something *I* don't understand. Someone made a magic-seeing ball to see *me*. To focus the ball, you have to include something that belongs to the person you're focusing it on. What could they have used that was mine?"

Eadric nodded. "That's a good question, but I have a better one. If you can't use magic, how are you going to turn us back? We can't hold hands all the way to Roc Mountain."

"Yeah," said Shelton. "And I want to go for a swim. Even freshwater is better than nothing."

"Don't worry," I said with more confidence than I felt. "I'll think of something."

Eight

"Would you look at this!" Eadric said, emerging ahead of me from a stand of trees that extended all the way to the water's edge. It had probably gone farther, but the bank had been washed away, carrying the trees that had been growing there with it. The sun had finally reached down into the valley while we were stumbling along the riverbank, making it possible to see the extent to which the river had grown during the night.

"What's wrong?" I asked, coming up behind him. Then I saw the river ahead and he didn't have to answer. An enormous pile of boulders that had long ago tumbled as far as the new riverbed blocked our way. Although it would have been easy to pass the day before, the river had continued to widen and now almost filled the valley from one side to the other.

Eadric used his free hand to gesture up ahead. "The best way to get to Roc Mountain is to follow this valley, but as it is now we can't walk along the river unless we turn into mountain goats. Flying would be better, but we'd have to use magic then, too. And since we can't use magic because the only way we'll get Bradston back is if we have surprise on our side . . ."

I let go of Eadric's hand and sat down abruptly, leaning against the trunk of a tree.

"Hey!" said Eadric. "Why'd you do that?"

I didn't want Eadric to see me looking as discouraged as I felt. Sometimes being invisible can be handy. "I need some time to think," I said, which was true as far as it went. I also needed some time to myself. The mess we were in was all my fault. If I had said a different spell to keep the trolls away from the men, or even one to limit the size of the river, we could have walked the length of the valley in half a day.

"Emma!" Eadric sounded alarmed. I glanced up but couldn't see him until he bumped my head with his hand. "Ah, there you are!" My distress must have shown on my face, because he dropped down beside me and took my hand in his. "What's wrong?" he asked.

"I've let you down," I said. "I feel terrible about it. I was supposed to get us to Bradston. Now I can't even get us to the end of the valley. I can't use my magic and there's no way else to . . ."

"Of course there's another way!" said Eadric. "That brook went through the valley and out the other end, which means that the river does, too. The ride might be rough, but I'm sure we can cobble together some sort of raft and let the river carry us there."

"That's a brilliant idea!" I said, and I kissed him full on the lips. "I don't know why I didn't think of it."

Eadric stood up, still holding my hand. "Because you've gotten in the habit of using your magic to solve our problems. But not every problem needs a magical solution."

It didn't take Eadric long to find fallen trees to form the floor of our raft. He lashed them together with vines, then made a makeshift rudder so we could steer it. The raft came apart twice as we dragged it to the water's edge, but he put it back together each time without complaining. After that, I didn't have the heart to tell him that it still didn't look very sturdy.

Once we had the raft by the water, it slipped in easily enough and we had to scramble to get on board. The logs started separating almost immediately, so we set to work tightening the lashing as best we could while trying to stay in physical contact with each other. Shelton didn't help much. He kept disappearing, and each time I was afraid he'd fallen overboard. Eadric finally got tired of my fretting and said, "If you're so worried about him, why don't you just make us visible again? I wish you would anyway. It's safe now—the trolls can't reach us here."

"We talked about this. If I use my magic, they'll see

that we're on the river and will know that we're headed toward the mountain. At least now they don't know where to look for us. And if we stay invisible, we might have a better chance of sneaking into the mountain and finding Bradston."

Eadric shrugged. "Suit yourself, but you're going to have to do it sooner or later."

The water had been smooth at first, but as the valley narrowed, the river coursed over rocks and boulders that had fallen in ages past. White water foamed around us as we rushed past plumes of spray and boulders too big for a giant to lift. We were fortunate at first because the raft hit a partly submerged rock and spun around, but didn't tip or come apart. The next time, however, it caught on something we couldn't see under the water, and we lost one of the logs. After that, we had to fight to hold the raft together. When it hit the next rock, the whole thing came apart, and I tumbled into the water headfirst.

Over the previous year and a half I'd become a very good swimmer—as a frog or a fish or even as a turtle. I hadn't done much swimming as a human, however, so I floundered in the water, trying to turn myself around and find Eadric and the remains of the raft before I was too far away to reach them. As my skirts weighed me down and caught on wedged branches and jagged rocks, I was tempted to turn myself into something, anything, that could fly or swim or . . .

"Emma!" Eadric shouted. "Where are you?"

"Over . . . here!" I spluttered as water washed over me. I looked wildly around, trying to find him in the foam, forgetting that he was still invisible, too.

"You have to turn us back now!" he shouted from a direction entirely different from where I'd been looking. "It's the only way I'll find you." Even if he'd been visible, the water was so rough that I might not have been able to see him in the churning waves.

"But . . . ," I began.

"No *buts*!" he shouted. "Just do it bef—"

When Eadric stopped talking, I nearly panicked. He must be underwater. What if he was seriously hurt? Forgetting the trolls and Bradston and everything but Eadric, I said the first visibility spell that I could think of.

"There you are!" said Eadric as we all became visible again. He was holding on to a log from our destroyed raft and was only a few yards away. Shelton was already climbing onto the log when Eadric towed it toward me. Grabbing the back of my gown in one fist, he dragged me to the log and held me until I'd draped myself over it.

"Thank you!" I gasped. "You don't know how happy I am to see you."

"About as happy as I am to see you," he said, and he kissed me.

"Don't you two ever let up?" grumbled Shelton from his perch atop the log.

We rode down the river holding on to the log while trying to stay in the channel and away from the rocks. Shelton strolled up and down, chattering and enjoying the spray. I saw Li'l overhead now and then, coming back to check on us before taking off again. When the river left the valley, the water spread out over a greater distance, becoming shallower in the process until our feet touched the ground. Eadric and I climbed out, abandoning our log. Shelton had crawled onto my shoulder, snagging my hair with his claws, but I didn't mind. I was too happy to be out of the river with Eadric to let anything bother me.

"That was fun!" said Shelton. "Can we do it again?"

Eadric snorted and sat on the ground to dump the water out of his boots. I wrung out my clothes as best I could, wishing that I could dry us both with a little magic.

"Now we head due north," Eadric said, patting Ferdy to make sure he was still there.

"I thought we were going east through Griffin Pass," I said.

"We were, but the rapids carried us past before I knew it. We don't have any choice now. We'll go north. I saw where the basilisks' caves were on the map, so we can avoid them altogether. As for the other beasts ... I'm sure Ferdy and I can handle them, whatever they are."

For the first few miles the landscape seemed normal enough, with scattered trees and scrub. Then the land abruptly changed as if we'd crossed a line and entered a completely different kingdom. The ground was dry and hard, and where there were rocks, they were shattered as if a giant had beaten them with a mighty club. There was evidence that wildflowers had once grown there as well as trees, but they were withered now, their leaves so dry that they rattled when the wind blew. From where we walked I could see small brown and white hills dotting the ground at uneven intervals. There was no sign of life, although I thought I heard a rooster crow.

We were approaching the first hill when I started to smell something awful. Eadric smelled it at the same time. "Where is that stench coming from?" he asked, making a face.

"I don't know, unless . . ." What had looked like a small hill from a distance was actually a dung heap nearly as high as my waist. The smell was so terrible that we had to hold our noses.

Shelton turned his eyestalks to examine it as we hurried past. "I'd hate to meet whatever did that!"

We continued on and soon saw a stone spire rising above the land. Perched on top was an enormous nest built from trees piled one on top of another. The nest sagged in places as if it were on the verge of falling apart. Shading his eyes against the glare of the sun, Eadric looked up and grunted. "Looks like a roc's nest, which explains the dung heaps. I've never been here before, but I've heard about this place. That pointy rock has been here for as long as anyone can remember, although the stories say that it wasn't always here. A witch planted it a long time ago, intending to build her home on the peak, then left when the people of Upper Montevista turned against her. Some say she was the reason that people in this kingdom don't like anyone who wields magic."

"I wonder what she did that was so awful," I said.

"I have no idea, but if you ask me, she couldn't have been a very smart witch. If she had been, she would have chosen a better spot to put her home—like on top of a mountain."

"Or in a swamp," I said.

"Or on the bottom of the ocean like Coral's palace," said Shelton, sounding wistful.

I patted the little crab with one finger. "Shelton, I think you're homesick."

"Who, me? Never!" said Shelton. "What's *homesick* mean?"

"It means you miss your home, like Emma misses Greater Greensward," said Eadric.

I smiled at him, pleased that he knew me so well.

Although the nest looked abandoned, we gave it a wide berth while trying to keep our bearings. Unfortunately, our path took us past more roc droppings and the awful smell.

We were passing another one when we saw toads using their front feet to roll eggs toward the dung heap.

"I don't know much about this kind of thing," said Shelton, "but is that normal?"

I gasped as the pieces of the puzzle came together. "Eadric," I said, "remember how your officer mentioned some other beasts that killed anyone who tried to pass through here? He didn't know what they were, but I think I do. If you see anything moving, don't look at it. And if you get a glimpse of something that looks like a snake or a rooster, look the other way. We're in a cockatrice breeding ground and we . . ."

"A what?" asked Shelton.

"I've never seen any before, but I've read about them in one of Grassina's bestiaries. That's a book that tells about different kinds of animals, Shelton," I told the little crab. "Cockatrices come from yolkless eggs that roosters have laid."

"I don't understand how a rooster can lay an egg, let alone one without a yolk," said Eadric.

"I don't either," I said. "I'm just telling you what I read. Anyway, toads take the eggs into dung heaps to hatch. And don't ask me why toads would care about the eggs, because I have no idea."

"And out comes one of those things you mentioned?" said Shelton.

Eadric nodded. "That's right. They have the head,

legs, and wings of a rooster and the body and tail of a snake. They're so ugly that you'll turn to stone if you look one in the eye. They can even shatter rock and wither plants with their ugliness."

"You're pulling my claw!" said Shelton. "There's no such thing . . . Is there?"

Eadric seemed to enjoy making Shelton nervous. "They're real, all right. I've heard that in some places people won't travel without a weasel. That's the only kind of animal cockatrices are afraid of, because weasels are immune to their gaze."

"I wish we had a weasel with us now," said Shelton, shifting from leg to leg.

"So do I," I said. Better yet, I wished I could turn us into weasels or maybe birds so we could fly away. But I couldn't risk any magic again. It was bad enough that I'd had to make us visible on the river. Not only had I used magic that could tell the trolls where we were, but I'd taken away whatever advantage we might have had by being invisible when there were cockatrices around. I could only hope that the trolls would think we had drowned.

"Just keep your eyes open," I told Eadric. "But don't look at anything."

We walked more carefully then, letting our eyes flick from one thing to the next without looking at anything for too long. There were more dung heaps beyond the spire, although only a few had toads near them. When

125

I saw movement out of the corner of my eye, I looked away, afraid of what I might see. "Look straight ahead," I told Eadric. "I think there's a cockatrice to our left."

I should have known better than to tell him, because the first thing he did was turn his head to look. "That's no cockatrice. It's just a big toad."

"I told you not to look!"

Eadric shrugged. "I won't when it's a cockatrice, but I can look at toads, can't I?"

He was so exasperating. "And how will you . . . Oh, never mind. Just keep your eyes straight ahead," I told him, missing my magic more than ever.

We came across our first cockatrice only a few minutes later. It was sunning itself on a pile of gravel, and I looked away as soon as I realized what it was. The creature was smaller than I'd expected and had a head more like a chick than a rooster. I hurried Eadric past it without telling him that it was there.

The cockatrice had seen us and wasn't about to let us go. "Yoo-hoo! I'm over here. Look at me!" it called in a high-pitched voice. "I can't believe it! You're acting as if I don't exist! You should see how beautiful I am. It isn't every day that someone gets to admire such magnificent plumage!"

"Keep going and pretend you didn't hear it," I whispered to Eadric.

I could hear the clack of tumbling gravel behind us,

but I didn't dare turn around. It stopped after we'd gone a few dozen feet.

As we continued on, we began to see previous cockatrice victims scattered across the barren ground. Men and trolls had been frozen in stone in various positions, some running, others raising their swords or clubs, a few even reaching to cover their eyes. We saw birds frozen with their wings spread, about to take off, while others lay broken on the ground, having frozen and fallen from the sky. It was an eerie setting, made more dangerous by the stone mice and insects that could trip the unwary.

The next cockatrice was waiting for us and had planted itself directly in our path. I looked away immediately, clapping my hand over Eadric's eyes. "Keep going!" I said. Turning aside, I tried to hustle him away from the little beast.

"I just wanted to say hello!" it cried in a plaintive voice. "You're missing a marvelous opportunity! I'm perfectly lovely and have so much to offer!"

"Most humans couldn't understand what it was saying," Eadric muttered.

"Exactly," I said. "And we have to pretend that we can't either."

That cockatrice followed us, too, although not as far as the first. We kept going, encountering one cockatrice after another, each one claiming to be beautiful. I was beginning to wonder if we would ever escape them entirely when Li'l found us again. "Hi, guys!" she said, startling me so that I let out a tiny shriek. "Sorry," she said. "I just came to see what you're doing."

"We're trying to get away from the cockatrices," said Shelton, sounding impatient.

"Then why are you running in circles?" asked Li'l. "Wouldn't it be better if you went straight ahead?"

"Circles?" I said in disbelief.

"Yeah. See, you're headed toward that pointy thing with the nest on top. Did you want to go back to the river?" Li'l tilted her wing in the direction we were going. The spire lay straight ahead, with the river running behind it in the distance.

"No," I said, and I pointed back the way we'd just come. "We want to go that way."

"So why aren't you?" Li'l asked.

"Good question," Eadric mumbled, but he stopped when I frowned at him.

"We want to, but we have to avoid the cockatrices. Give me a minute to think," I said. I considered asking Li'l to lead us out, but she shouldn't look at a cockatrice any more than we should. Eadric had mentioned a weasel, but we didn't have one, so that was out. I'd heard that a cockatrice would freeze if it saw its own reflection. Unfortunately, we didn't have a mirror with us. I thought about the cockatrices we'd come across. None of them

128

was very big or very fearsome, maybe because they all seemed to be young. Each one had followed us for a time, although not for very long. Maybe, like a lot of other animals, they were territorial. *And maybe,* I thought, tapping my cheek with my finger, *they have a reason to be.*

"I want to try something," I said. "You three stay here with your eyes shut. No matter what you hear, don't open them until I tell you to, understand?"

Eadric frowned. "What are you going to do?"

"Nothing any more dangerous than what we've already been doing. Remember what I said. No matter what you hear . . ."

"We know," said Eadric, "although I should be the one to lead us out of here."

I left Shelton and Li'l perched on Eadric's shoulders, something none of them was happy about, and walked a short distance toward the spire. Keeping my eyes shut, I called out in a loud voice, "I wish I could see that really beautiful cockatrice. The one I passed a little while ago. I think it was the most beautiful cockatrice in the world, but I have to see it again to be sure."

From every direction there came the scratching of claws on gravel as the cockatrices overcame their natural reluctance to leave their territory. Bragging about their beauty, they kept coming until I could hear that they were only a few feet away. "Now stop!" I said, holding up my hand. "There are so many of you that I'm going to need your help in deciding. Please turn to your neighbor and take a good long look, then tell me which one of you is the most beautiful."

I heard the sound of feathers rustling, and then the cockatrices all began to talk at once. "She must mean me!"

"No, I'm sure I'm—"

"Anyone can tell that I—"

The chorus of excited voices was loud at first, but as one cockatrice after another looked at its neighbor and turned to stone, the voices dwindled into silence. I never did hear which was the most beautiful, but by keeping my eyes straight ahead I was able to find Eadric and finally leave the cockatrice breeding ground for good. My only regret was that we couldn't take one of the little monsters with us to use against the trolls.

Nine

We left the shattered land just as abruptly as we'd entered it. With one step we went from gravel and sand to lush grass that felt soft beneath our feet. Ahead of us lay a mixed forest of spruce and leaf-bearing trees, with Roc Mountain rising in the distance. It was an oddly shaped mountain, which, according to Eadric, people thought looked like a roc, although no one had ever seen any of the giant birds on it. The forest lapping at its base looked welcoming in the late afternoon heat. Like a thirsty man who sees an oasis in the desert, we hurried toward the trees and the shade they offered. Cool air washed over us as we stepped beneath the green canopy. Eadric and I sighed with relief and sat down in the shade to rest while Li'l settled on the branch of a tree.

We hadn't gotten much sleep the night before, and I couldn't make myself go any farther. Although our stomachs rumbled with hunger, we fell asleep, dozing against a tree's rough bark. We would have slept longer than we did, but Shelton grew tired of waiting for us. "Get up!" he said, pinching me hard enough to raise a welt on the back of my hand. "We have places to go and a prince to rescue."

"You didn't have to do that," I said, rubbing my hand.

Eadric was rubbing a similar welt on the arm he'd had around my shoulder. "I'm hungry," he said. "Why don't I start a fire and cook a crab for supper?"

"Ha, ha! Very funny," Shelton said, not sounding at all amused. He skittered down my leg, then turned to face Eadric with his claws clacking. "You can't eat me!" he said. "I'd pinch you really hard if you tried. And if you did . . . why, I'd be all stringy and taste really bad and . . ."

I scooped up the little crab and set him on my shoulder. "Don't worry. I won't let him eat you."

"I wouldn't be so sure about that," Eadric told Shelton while helping me to my feet. "She has to sleep sometime."

"Stop it, you two," I said, losing my patience. "We have enough to worry about without you fighting."

"You heard her," said Shelton, but he quieted down when I poked him.

Li'l flew overhead to keep us on course while Eadric and I made our way through the forest. We were both hungry, so we stopped to look for berries in the few likely spots we came across, but didn't find anything edible.

When I heard the first rumble of thunder, I thought it was Eadric's stomach. It wasn't until the wind picked up, waving the branches overhead and making the leaves rustle like rushing water, that I knew a storm was approaching.

"Li'l!" I called into the darkening sky. "Can you look for some kind of shelter? A cave or hut would be fine."

"I'll see what I can find!" she called back, as she disappeared into the gloom.

When she finally met up with us again, she led us through the woods in a new direction. We covered our heads and ran as the wind grew stronger and loose leaves and twigs fell on us like hail. The rain had just started to pelt us when we came to the clearing she had found and saw the remains of a long-deserted castle. Lightning ripped the sky, lighting up the clearing, then thunder boomed, and a tree cracked, splitting in the forest behind us. The smell of sulfur soured the air, and I could feel my hair stand on end as Eadric grabbed my hand and ran.

Lightning blazed again. I stumbled and would have fallen if Eadric hadn't been holding my hand. He pulled me through the gateway, over the ruined portcullis, and across the cracked and broken paving stones of the courtyard. The wind was whipping my hair into stinging strands that bit my cheeks when Eadric dragged me up the steps and past a sagging door. It was dark inside, lit only by the lightning flashes showing through the doorway and the narrow windows set high on the walls. We had stepped directly into the Great Hall, empty except for some old, rickety tables and a massive fireplace too crumbled to use.

While Eadric tried to find a torch with enough oil left to burn, Li'l took off to explore on her own and I began to look around the Hall. Shelton rode my shoulder like my own miniature knight ready to protect me with his claws.

The storm moved on, but we were fortunate that Eadric had found a torch and some candle stubs that smelled of rancid fat. He lit the torch easily enough with a flint he always carried, and we began to explore together. The castle was in a terrible state, its walls crumbling and even missing in some sections where the roots of trees had forced their way in. The few pieces of furniture that we saw were broken or rotting, the scraps of tapestries black with mold. Rats had taken over the kitchen, gnawing everything that wasn't stone or metal and fouling the rest. Certain that we wouldn't find anything to eat, we didn't look for food. Instead we headed upstairs to find a place to sleep.

We were in a hallway on the second floor when Li'l stopped by to make sure that we were all right, then left in search of her own dinner, an easy task for an insect-eating bat. I remembered my days as a bat and thought of all the meals I'd enjoyed that I couldn't stomach as a human. Eadric had been thinking about food as well. "When we get Bradston home to my parents, I'm going to insist that they have a feast. We'll have roast venison, eel stew, fruit tarts, and aged cheese . . ."

"That isn't helping," I said. "You're just making me hungrier."

Eadric sighed. "I don't think I could get any hungrier than I am now."

Although the castle had been so silent after the storm that we could hear each other breathe, the wind began to howl again, coming closer as if it were inside the castle itself. I was reaching for Eadric's hand for comfort when an apparition dressed in gray flew into the corridor, her long, white hair streaming behind her. Eadric's hand met mine and I gripped it so tightly that it probably hurt. Whatever she was, this creature terrified me just by being there. It wasn't so much her red, sunken eyes and gaunt features that made her frightening; there was an air about her of great sorrow and hopelessness that turned my knees to jelly while making me want to flee. I was hoping that she would pass us by, but she saw us and stopped to float above our heads. Eadric shoved me behind him, and I could feel that his skin had turned cold and clammy.

"Oh, woe is me!" she wailed. "What evil has come to pass on this most dreadful of days? Invaders have come to this forsaken castle, here to disturb the peaceful slumber of . . ."

Eadric stuck out his chin and said in as brave a voice as he could manage, "What are you going on about, banshee? If you mean us, we're not invaders. We came here to get out of the storm."

Of course she's a banshee, I thought, mentally kicking myself for not recognizing her from the descriptions I'd heard. Only someone with the power of a banshee could have made me feel such overwhelming despair.

When the banshee smiled, her eyes sparkled, and she didn't look nearly as scary. "You mean you aren't here for some nefarious reason?" she said. "Then welcome, you poor things! I'm so glad you're here! I never get to talk to anyone except when I'm working, and then I'm supposed to say things like, 'Woe is me' and 'Beware' and 'Uncle Rupert is going to die.' And then they look at me like I have two heads, which I don't because I'm not a troll, and they always say, 'Oh, no, the banshee is here!' Do you know how that makes me feel? Every time I show up, people run screaming and warn everybody else that I'm around. Believe me, I've thought about staying home and sleeping late, but I can't because I care about people. Without me to warn them, people would die unexpectedly, and then where would their relatives be? When I tell them, they have time to make arrangements, say good-bye . . . you know—important things. I'm actually a very nice person; it's just that no one gives me a chance to prove it."

"Sorry to hear that," I said, not knowing what else to say.

"Thanks," she said, her smile becoming even more brilliant. I began to wonder why I'd found her so frightening.

She glanced at Eadric and blinked. "You're looking at my teeth, aren't you? Pardon me," she said, and she stuck her finger in her mouth. "Darn bugs! But that's what I get for flying around with my mouth open." Raking the fingers of her other hand through her hair, she frowned when she found a snarl. "I must look a fright. Do you know what flying all day does to your hair? It's going to take hours to get all the knots out. Say, you don't have a cucumber on you, do you? I've heard that cucumber slices feel refreshing on your eyes." The banshee yawned until her jaw made a cracking sound. "I am *so* tired! I've got to go to bed. Choose whatever rooms you'd like and I'll see you in the morning." Rubbing her already red eyes, she drifted past us down the hall.

When Eadric pulled me into his arms and held me tight, I could feel that he was shaking. "That's such a relief!" he murmured into my hair. "I thought she was here to make one of her announcements. The last time I saw a banshee was the day my grandfather died from a hunting accident. A banshee came before we knew that his injuries were serious. When I saw her tonight, I thought it meant that I was going to lose you. I couldn't bear that, Emma." He kissed me on the lips before I could reply, a tender kiss that banished the last of any despair I'd felt from the banshee.

"At least this banshee turned out to be nice," I said when I could talk again. "I didn't really want to go looking for someplace else to sleep."

Shelton tickled my neck with his eyestalks. "Are you going to stand around all night and talk about sleeping, or are you actually going to do something about it? I'm so tired I can hardly hold up my eyes."

"All right then," said Eadric. "Let's see what these rooms look like."

Exhausted, we chose the first two rooms we could find that had solid walls and no holes in the floors or ceilings. From the ragged bed curtains and the rotting tapestries on the walls we could tell that they had once belonged to members of a noble family. Eadric left a sputtering candle on the floor, then went to his room while I set Shelton beside the candle.

"Wow!" he said. "The floor in here is soft. What is this stuff?"

I touched the floor, then rubbed my fingers together. "It's just dust."

"Ick!" he said, picking his legs up one at a time and shaking them. "This place is worse than the room Eadric's mother stuck you in. At least that one was clean."

I blew out the candle and crawled across the

musty-smelling bed. "Yes, but the banshee's nicer than Eadric's mother." The little crab was still puttering around the floor when I lay down and pulled the blanket scraps over me.

Although most castles were cold and damp, the banshee's castle was the worst I'd ever visited. It had been years since fires had heated the fireplaces, and the cold clung to every surface. I lay shivering under threadbare blankets that wouldn't have been fit for my father's hounds, waiting for my body heat to warm the mildew-stained fabric. When I finally drifted off, I slept fitfully and woke at every little sound. I didn't succumb to a restful sleep until the sun came up, heating the air through the one narrow window.

The next time I woke, Eadric was sitting on the edge of my bed, gazing at me. "I didn't want to wake you. You looked so peaceful lying there."

"Have you seen Li'l?" I asked, rubbing my eyes.

Eadric reached down to brush a lock of hair from my cheek. "She stopped by to check on us, then went outside to look around. She says this castle is too creepy even for her. It is pretty bad," he said, looking around the room. "We shouldn't stay any longer than we have to. We'll say good-bye if we see the banshee, then be on our way."

I felt a slight tug on the blanket and looked down to

139

see Shelton clambering up the side of the bed. "The sooner we're out of here, the better," he said. "I think I'm allergic to dust."

My stomach rumbled loudly enough for everyone to hear. "Maybe the banshee has some food," I said.

"Would you really want to eat whatever a banshee eats?" asked Eadric.

"Maybe," said Shelton. "But I won't know until I see it. Why are we wasting our time here?"

We found the banshee in the Great Hall sipping from a mug. She looked much better than she had the night before. Although her skin was still pale and her cheeks were gaunt, her eyes were a nice shade of brown instead of blood red, her hair was braided and covered with a light veil like my mother often wore, and her voice wasn't nearly as screechy as it had been the night before.

"I want to thank you for your hospitality," I told the banshee. "That was a terrible storm last night. I don't know what we would have done if we hadn't come across your castle."

"Pah!" she said. "Don't thank me. Having you here is such a treat. It's nice to talk to someone who isn't blubbering in her sleeve." The banshee set her mug on the table with a click. "That's something I don't understand. Why do they have to be so gloomy? If I were about to die, I wouldn't want to spend my last hours around people who were moaning and tearing their hair out. I'd want to laugh and have a good time." She sighed and ran her fingertip around the rim of her mug. "But that's just me. Maybe some people like being mournful. I do it because I have to. It's part of my job."

Shelton had taken refuge in my sleeve when I'd come down the stairs. Trying to get my attention, he pinched me, hard. "Ow!" I said, more startled than hurt. When the banshee looked at me quizzically, I pulled the little crab out of my sleeve and set him on the table. "This is Shelton. He's a friend of ours."

"Aren't you the dearest little thing!" said the banshee, bending down for a closer look. "I've never seen anything like you before. You must be very special."

"Oh, I am," he said, raising his eyestalks to look at her. "I normally live in the ocean with a mermaid named Coral, but she had to go away, so I'm visiting Princess Emma and Prince Eadric. We went to visit Upper Montevista, but Eadric's brother had been kidnapped. I'm helping them find the boy now."

"Your brother is missing?" she asked, turning to Eadric. "Is that why you're here?"

I glanced at Eadric, not wanting to tell the banshee more than he was willing to share. He shrugged as if to say, "why not?" so I told her about the trolls kidnapping Bradston. "We're on our way to the troll queen's home," I said. "It isn't far from here, is it?"

"No," said the banshee. "Not if you know where

141

you're headed. Follow the row of pine trees to the village, then go straight through to the edge of the forest. The entrance is easy to see. I've never been inside, but I've seen it with my mirror. I check my mirror every day so I'll know who's about to die. Sometimes when I look at it, I hear people talking about the troll queen. They say that she's evil and enjoys destroying whatever she touches. She tortures her victims before eating them." The banshee glanced at Eadric. "And you say she has your little brother? That poor defenseless boy. You must feel so sorry for him, living his last hours in the hands of that horrible monster."

"That's why we're in a hurry," said Eadric. "We want to get him out of there as soon as we can."

The banshee bit her lip, then said, "I know what we should do! We'll ask my magic mirror to show us what your brother is doing. Although in all good conscience, I have to tell you that no one who isn't a troll has ever gone into the queen's caverns and come out alive. But we'll take a look and then we'll know for sure."

The banshee kept the mirror in her bedchamber, an even gloomier room than the ones in which we'd slept. The bed hangings were tattered shreds, as faded a gray as her gown. There were no tapestries on the cold, stone walls, and the draft was much worse because of the gaping hole where the ceiling had partially collapsed. I didn't see any sign of torches or candles, so perhaps she didn't need them.

Eadric didn't seem to have noticed any of this, having gone straight to the mirror. "How does it work?" he asked, prodding the mirror's frame.

"You don't need to touch it," the banshee hurried to say when it wobbled on its stand. "Step back and you'll see."

Eadric and I stayed off to one side while the banshee stood in front of the mirror and announced loudly, "I want to see Prince Bradston of Upper Montevista."

The surface of the mirror rippled and the banshee's reflection disappeared. A boy came into view, lying on a bier surrounded by gibbering, prancing trolls. Blood dripped from the bier, and it was obvious that the child no longer lived. It was very convincing, but something about it was not quite right. Although the boy looked like Bradston, he looked too sweet, too innocent, too different from the Bradston I'd met. I'd been around him only briefly, but I knew with a certainty that the Bradston in the mirror was not the real one.

Eadric gasped. "No!" he said. "That can't be possible!" I put my arms around him and held him close.

"You see, Eadric," said the banshee, her voice filled with pain. "There's no hope for him. Your brother is already gone. It's no use trying to rescue him."

"That can't be right," I said, shaking my head. "I don't think that's really Bradston. Ask the mirror again, but tell it to show you the truth. I don't use magic mirrors myself, but I've been told that they aren't always reliable, especially when they get older."

"Oh, I'm sure this mirror is right," said the banshee. "It was given to me when I became a banshee. It has to be right every time."

"How old is it?" I asked.

The banshee shrugged. "At least a few hundred years, I expect."

"Then it may not be accurate anymore. Please try it again," I said. "We really need to know about Bradston."

The banshee looked from me to the mirror and back. "I suppose it won't hurt to try, although it's just going to show us the same thing again. Mirror, show us the truth about Prince Bradston of Upper Montevista. As he actually is this very minute."

The image of the boy and the dancing trolls disappeared and a gray fog swirled in its place, fading away to show three figures seated on the floor of a small cave. The picture grew larger as if we were moving closer to them until they looked as though they were in the room with us.

"There's Bradston," I said, "and those must be some of his captors." Two trolls sat beside the boy, who was laughing so hard that he had to hold his sides. The trolls seemed uncomfortable, as if they didn't understand what was going on but didn't like it nonetheless.

Eadric laughed out loud. "Now *that's* Bradston. He's making fun of the trolls. He's probably teasing them about something they've done. I should know. He's acted that way around me often enough."

"How is that possible?" asked the banshee. "He was dead in the other image. How do I know which one is right?"

"I'm sure the second one is. The boy in it is acting like the real Bradston," said Eadric.

The banshee wrung her hands. "Yes, but what about all the images I've seen over the years? Those people were about to die. I went to warn their families and they did die, just like I'd foreseen. But if there are two images . . . Is it possible that they wouldn't have died if they hadn't been expecting to because of what I'd said? This is terrible! What am I going to do now? If they died because of something that I did . . ." Wailing and tearing at her hair, the banshee fled down the hall as the image faded from the mirror.

Eadric took my hand in his and turned it over to kiss my palm. "Thank you for showing me the real Bradston. That first image had me convinced that he was dead."

"I know," I said. "I almost believed it myself. Those poor people, if what she said was true . . ."

Eadric shuddered. "Let's get out of here before she comes back. I shouldn't have believed her, but lies are harder to discount coming from a magic mirror. I prefer fighting trolls to listening to a banshee. Ferdy and I can handle trolls just fine," he said, patting his sword again.

"I'm sure you can," I said, and I turned my head so he wouldn't see my smile.

Ten

It was nearly noon when we left the banshee's castle. We started out by following the row of pine trees that she'd mentioned. Stone markers showed that an old road had once run beside them, but it had long since fallen into disuse and was mostly overgrown. Because we still couldn't find anything to eat, we continued walking long after we normally would have stopped. When darkness fell and the pine trees melted into the rest of the forest, we asked Li'l for help. She was happy to lead us and flew off to look around.

The night was well along when we reached the village that Li'l had found, making the few candles still burning in the windows a welcome sight. Grouped around a small central field, a cluster of narrow houses with steeply pitched roofs had been built so close to each other that they seemed to present a united front to the surrounding forest. Only a narrow gap separated the houses, leaving barely enough room for two people to walk side by side.

"I hope there's an inn here," said Eadric. "And I hope they're still serving supper."

I yawned and brushed my hair out of my eyes. "And I hope they have some rooms available after we've eaten."

"I hope they have a nice bucket of water," Shelton said from inside my sleeve. "And maybe a little salt to add to it."

"I'll see you later," said Li'l. "I don't like inns. There are always too many people there who like to hit bats."

After walking the length of the path that led between the houses without seeing an inn or anyone to talk to, Eadric declared, "We're not sleeping outside tonight. This village is too close to the troll's mountain. Anything could be in these woods." Picking the closest house, he rapped on the door with his knuckles. The thump was so loud in the otherwise silent night that I was sure everyone in the village must have heard it.

I gasped when a man stepped out of the shadows only a few feet away. "May I help you?" he asked with an odd accent to his words. The light from the windows did little more than outline his shape in the gloom, and I couldn't help but feel uneasy.

"We're seeking lodging for the night," said Eadric, stepping between me and the man. "Is there an inn close by?"

The man chuckled, but it wasn't a pleasant sound. "No inns that you could reach tonight. However, I have some empty rooms that I let out to travelers. Will it be just the two of you?"

"Yes," said Eadric, placing his hand on Ferdy's hilt. Apparently I wasn't the only one who felt ill at ease around the stranger. "And if we could arrange for supper as well . . ."

"Of course," said the man. "I'm sure my wife can come up with something."

I took Eadric's hand as the man led us to the largest house in the village. As narrow as the others, it was two stories tall with a pair of windows on the upper floor that looked out over the street. Despite the candles flickering in the windows, it didn't look as if anyone were home. I drew back when the door opened to a dank, earthy smell that seemed out of place indoors. "Are you all right?" whispered Eadric as he tucked my arm in his.

"Yes," I said, "but this house—"

"Right this way," said the man, leading us into the large front room. A table had been set with two trenchers and two mugs as if we'd been expected. I looked around, thinking we were alone in the silent house, and was surprised to see a grizzled old man watching us from the corner by the hearth. "My neighbor, Humphrey," said our host, who I could now see was fair-haired with pale skin and piercing blue eyes. There was a whisper of sound, and a young woman with the same coloring stepped into the doorway of another room. "And this is my wife, Sulie. She'll see to your needs. My name is Corbin. Please sit. Sulie will have your supper ready soon." With a nod to his wife, the man disappeared out the front door.

We took our seats as the woman set a pitcher of ale on the table. "I'll have the food ready in just a minute," she said. "Drink plenty of this nice stout ale. It builds up the blood."

"Aye, that it does," said Humphrey as Sulie left the room. "That ale is good for you. I've had my fair share over the years and I'm still here." He laughed when he said this as if at a private joke. "Where do you hail from?" he asked, wiping his eyes.

"I'm from Greater Greensward." Wondering if I should tell him about Eadric, I glanced across the table and knew right away that my prince wasn't going to be any help. He was downing his ale as if he hadn't had anything to drink in days, and didn't seem to be paying attention to anything else.

It wasn't until the young woman set clay bowls in front of us that Eadric looked up. "Here you go," said Sulie. "This'll put meat on your bones and thicken your blood."

"Looks good, doesn't it?" said Humphrey, but he was looking at me, not the food.

The bowls held a thick stew filled with some kind of meat and chunks of vegetables. I'd given up eating meat after I'd turned into an animal the first time, but I was too hungry to go without eating anything. Swallowing the chunks of carrots and potatoes as fast as I could, I tried not to think about their meat-soaked flavor. Eadric, however, had no such problem. After finishing his stew, he reached for what remained of mine. While he ate, I chanced to look around the room and caught the old man watching me. I fidgeted under his gaze until Eadric had scraped my bowl clean.

"Eadric," I said under my breath. "Perhaps we could see about those bedchambers now."

Sulie had already left the room, but Humphrey must have heard me, because he called to the young woman, saying, "They want to go to bed!"

"Of course you do," she said to us, wiping her hands on her apron as she came out of the room in the back. "You must be tired after such a long walk. I'm sure you won't have any problem falling asleep."

"How do you know we walked a long way?" Eadric asked, quirking an eyebrow.

"Because everywhere is a long way from here," Sulie replied, laughing. "Now, if you'll follow me . . ."

Eadric glanced at the empty bowls. "I wasn't finished eating."

Sulie shrugged, saying "I'm sorry, but that's all there is. We weren't expecting company." Then turning to me, she added, "Your lad has a hearty appetite! I like that in a man."

Humphrey laughed again, and I could feel his gaze

on my back as I started up the creaky stairs. He'd made me uncomfortable, although I couldn't say why, so I was relieved when we reached the landing and the old man could no longer see us.

There were four doors on the second floor and Sulie showed us to two of them. Neither of the rooms was very big. Eadric gave me the larger one, but was soon back, knocking on my door. I let him in, wondering what he could have to say now when he hadn't spoken a word during supper.

"I think you should come to the other room," he said. "Its window is small and has a shutter on it. The bed will be easier to move, too."

"Do you want to trade rooms?" I asked, not sure what he was saying.

"Not at all. I'll stay there, too. I think I can defend it better if it comes to that."

"Defend?" I said. "What makes you think you'll need to?"

"Because something's not quite right about this place. Did you notice that there are no roads going in or out? And I think it's odd that ordinary people would want to live so close to the trolls' mountain. I wouldn't be surprised if they have some sort of agreement worked out with the troll queen. Maybe they tell her about everyone who's passing through, or maybe they turn them over to the trolls in exchange for their own safety. Those stories about trolls killing travelers are true, you know."

"And you think shutters would keep us safe?" I asked.

Eadric shrugged. "They're better than nothing."

"Fine," I said. "But I get the bed. All I want is a good night's sleep."

We were about to leave the room when Li'l flew in through the open window. "There you are!" she said, landing on my shoulder. She was out of breath and I could feel her little heart pounding.

"What have you been up to?" I asked, following Eadric from the room.

"I was looking for bats," said Li'l. "I just wanted to meet them and ask if they knew anything about the troll queen. The whole village smells like them, but I couldn't find a single one."

"That's odd," I said. "Where do you think they went?"

"I don't know. That's why I was looking for so long. This is a nice room," she said as we stepped into the other chamber. "It reminds me of a cave."

"Yeah," said Eadric. "Me, too." The room was small and dark, with one tiny window and a narrow bed. It was situated over the room where we'd eaten, and I could hear people talking below us. "I closed the shutters," Eadric continued. "I'm going to push the bed in front of the door to block it."

"Why?" asked Li'l. "What are you afraid of?"

"Eadric thinks the people in the village might have told the trolls about us," I replied.

"Really?" Li'l fluttered to the window and landed on the sill. "Then we should take turns watching." The little bat shuffled from one side to the other, peering through the cracks in the shutters.

I helped Eadric move the bed. We were shoving it against the door when a clock somewhere in the village chimed midnight. "Did you hear that?" I asked.

"You mean the clock?" said Eadric.

"No, what came after it. They were talking downstairs, but they stopped when the clock chimed. They didn't stop when it chimed before. Wait!" I held up one finger to silence him, listened for a moment, and said, "Humphrey just said, 'It's time,' but he didn't say what it was time for."

Eadric looked puzzled. "How can you hear that?"

"I needed to talk to a butterfly a few days ago, so I had to have extra-sharp hearing."

"Uh-huh," said Eadric. "I believe that, coming from you. Maybe when he said, 'It's time,' he meant it was time to go to bed."

I cocked my head to listen. The stairs creaked as someone climbed them, just as they had for us. "Maybe, except . . ." The creaking grew louder and I could hear a difference. "There are more people now. At least five or six."

"Would you look at that," Li'l said, peering out the window again. "All those people are coming this way."

I edged past the bed to peek out the crack in the shutters. It was true. The doors of the village had been thrown open, and everyone was heading toward the house where we were staying.

"*Psst,* Emma," whispered Eadric. "Look at that."

I turned away from the window. Someone was on the other side of the door trying to push it open, but it barely moved an inch before smacking into the bed.

"Whatever you do," I told Eadric, "don't open the door. I have a bad feeling about this."

Whoever was on the other side hesitated, then tapped on the door and said in a pleasant voice, "It's me. Corbin. I've come to see if you need more blankets. Just ask me in and I'll give them to you."

"We're fine," I said. "The night is warm."

"I've brought you another candle as well."

"We don't need another candle. We'll be going to sleep soon," I said.

"Then open the door and we can have a nice chat about what you'd like for breakfast."

"Maybe we should . . . ," said Eadric.

"Don't you dare move!" I spat at him, then called to our host, "There's no need. Whatever you normally make would be fine."

Something scrabbled at the shutters, sounding like a

mouse in the walls. "Emma," said Li'l. "I think you'd better see this."

"What is it now?" I muttered, bending down to peer out the crack again. I couldn't see at first, because something was in the way. Then it moved and the moonlight showed me a man floating in midair, poking ineffectually at the shutters. There were other people there as well, people who would have seemed normal if they hadn't been floating outside a second-floor window.

"Are those people supposed to have teeth like that?" Li'l whispered, peering out the shutter beside me.

"Only if they're vampires," I whispered back. They were fangs, not teeth really, and they looked out of place on the middle-aged woman and the little girl who leered at the shutters as if they knew we were watching from inside.

"Come join us," called the woman. "We'll have a party and you'll be the guests of honor!"

"I bet," I muttered, and then I turned to my friends. "Don't worry. We're safe in here. Garrid told me that vampires can't come in unless they're invited. Just don't open the door or the window. We'll be able to leave in the morning when they go to sleep."

"Some of them are bats," Li'l said. "Or at least they are now."

A cool, dank vapor filtered into the room through the shutters. I peeked out again. Sure enough, there were bats outside flying side by side with the floating vampires. I was still watching when there was another puff of cool, dank air and a little old lady with a kindly face turned into a bat.

Corbin, or whoever was on the other side of the door, started knocking loudly, demanding to be invited in. Eadric faced the door with his arms crossed and his legs braced as if awaiting the onslaught of an army. Convinced that no one was about to come through that door, I turned back to the window in time to see Li'l struggling to open it.

"What are you doing?" I said, slapping the shutter closed again.

"Didn't you see him? Garrid has come looking for me. I have to go to him!"

I shook my head and bent down to take a peek. "That's not possible. How could he be here?"

"Did she say that Garrid's here?" asked Eadric. "We could use another strong arm. Maybe we should let him in."

I turned back to Eadric in disbelief. "Another strong arm that happens to belong to a vampire? I don't think so. He may be Li'l's mate, but do you really think he'd side against a village full of . . . Li'l, wait! What are you doing?"

In the moment that I'd had my back turned, Li'l had pulled the shutter open enough that she could squeeze her tiny body through. As I watched in horror, she darted into the night sky and was lost in a flurry of bat wings and jubilant voices.

"Li'l!" I cried out, but she was gone . . . and back again in an instant with a familiar bat in tow. It *was* Garrid. If I hadn't been a bat before myself, I never would have recognized him, but I'd learned to tell the difference on more than one frosty night excursion. Garrid was a particularly handsome bat, just as he was an exceedingly handsome man.

"Emma, quick!" shouted Li'l. "Let us in!"

I couldn't lose my little friend, not after all we'd been through together, so I opened the window just wide enough to let her in and . . . in came a flood of bats, all of them vampires except one.

Two bats whispered sweet nothings into each other's ears. The rest came straight for Eadric and me.

"What the . . . !" shouted Eadric as a cloud of bats covered him from head to toe. I could see him fighting them off as a similar wave knocked me away from the window, against the bed, then down to the floor. My first thought was that Garrid had betrayed us. The second was that I'd have to use magic to save my Eadric. I was holding my arms in front of my throat, trying to fend off their fangs while furiously working on a spell, when a voice shouted, "Off them! They're my friends!" and all the bats fell away.

It was suddenly so quiet in the room that I could hear Eadric's ragged breath as I tried to catch my own. I sat up, jerking my hand away when it touched the leathery skin of a bat. Then a firm grip enclosed my fingers, and Garrid the man was helping me to my feet. "Sorry about that," he said before turning to Eadric. "It didn't occur to me that they'd follow me, but you know how it goes. Invite one vampire in and they think it means everyone's welcome."

"Then it wasn't a trick?" I asked.

"Emma, how could you?" cried Li'l. "Garrid would never do such a thing. He came looking for me."

"Uh, Li'l," Garrid said, scratching his head and looking sheepish. "I didn't know you were here. It wasn't until I heard your voice that I knew it was you."

"Then why are you here?" she asked, fluttering to the bed. "I bet I know! You were visiting friends and heard my voice and came to protect me. That was it, wasn't it?"

"Actually, I arrived only a few minutes ago. I was delayed at my last stop. That was family business, too, just like this. As the oldest member of the family, I have to give my permission before anyone can marry, so I stop by every few months to see if anyone is engaged. It's a tradition, you understand, but tradition is very important when you live as long as we do."

"You mean these people are your relatives?" I asked.

Garrid nodded. "On my mother's side. Second cousins six times removed, that kind of thing."

"Why didn't you tell me?" Li'l asked. "I would have loved to have come with you."

Garrid looked even more sheepish than before. "It didn't occur to me. I've been making the rounds for hundreds of years and I've never had a wife to bring before."

"A wife!" shouted one of the bats. There was another puff of dank air and the bat turned into the grizzled old man who had sat beside us at supper. "Why didn't you send word that you had married! We'd about given up hope that you ever would! And what is your name, young lady?" he asked, extending his hand to Li'l.

Li'l looked flustered at first, then pulled her wings close to her body. I could tell she was upset. "I'm not a young lady. I'm a bat," she said in a tiny voice.

The old man looked surprised at first, but he quickly recovered himself and smiled down at where she sat on the bed. "And a beautiful bat, too," he told Li'l. "I must say, Garrid, you've found yourself a lovely wife."

"I know I have," said Garrid. "But thank you for saying so. And now I'd like to invite you all to an unexpectedly joyous celebration. I want you to have the chance to meet my wife and our dear friends Prince Eadric and Princess Emeralda." All the vampires in the room began to talk at once, excited at the prospect of a party even if it didn't involve drinking our blood. "You'll have to tell me later why you're here," he told me. "I know it wasn't because you were looking for me."

"I will," I said, "although you'll have to excuse us from your celebration. You're used to staying up, but we have to leave in the morning. All I want to do now is sleep for the rest of the night, undisturbed."

"We'll see what we can arrange," he said, smiling down at me.

A short time later, Eadric and I were in the room that was supposed to have been mine. While he slept on the floor with Ferdy by his side, I lay curled up in the bed sleeping peacefully with Shelton keeping watch from my pillow. Boards had been nailed over the window and on the door hung a sign that read,

NO ONE IS WELCOME,
SO DO NOT DISTURB!

Eleven

Li'l was unusually quiet when we started out the next morning. She had celebrated with Garrid and his relatives all night, but she usually stayed up until dawn, so I knew she wasn't acting that way because she was extra tired. When Garrid offered to accompany us after hearing about our mission, she looked more upset than pleased.

The two of them took turns flying above the trees to make sure we were headed in the right direction and to tell us how to get around obstacles such as bottomless pits and werewolf dens. The first time Li'l left and came back, she landed on my shoulder and stayed there until it was her turn again. She sat with her wings covering her head, another sign that she wasn't happy. Garrid, on the other hand, laughed and joked when he wasn't flying, alternating between riding on Eadric's shoulder and mine. I knew that he was aware of Li'l's bad mood, however, because he kept trying to get her to talk to him and told

162

funny stories to try to make her laugh. After a while he gave up and sat in puzzled silence, glancing at her now and then.

Garrid wasn't the only one who was worried. We'd been walking for a few hours when something occurred to me. "Eadric," I said. "What if the troll queen guessed that we're in the forest? She could be surrounding it right now, waiting for us to come out."

Eadric snorted. "I doubt it. Haven't you seen how big this forest is? More likely they'd figure out where we were going and wait by the entrance."

"Is that supposed to make me feel better? Because it doesn't."

"Don't worry," he said, patting Ferdy. "Between the two of us, we can take care of anything. I wish you'd have a little faith."

"I would," I muttered under my breath, "if we weren't talking about trolls. I've seen what they can do."

"Bradston looked good when we saw the truth in the mirror, didn't he? That boy can even give trolls a hard time," Eadric said with a hint of pride in his voice.

"He looked fine, although his skin seemed a little odd. Your mother said that he was sick. Did she ever tell you what was wrong with him?" I asked.

Eadric shrugged. "I assumed she meant that he had a cold. My mother makes a fuss over the smallest sniffle."

"He didn't look like they hurt him or anything," I said.

"They'd better not," growled Eadric. "He's my little brother, and if anyone is going to hurt him because he was stupid enough to fall into the hands of trolls, it's going to be me."

⟳

It hadn't taken long for Li'l and Garrid to find the entrance to the trolls' caves, but then, they were bats, after all. As we neared the edge of the woods, it was Li'l's turn to check our position, and she came back only a few minutes after leaving. "There are trolls up ahead, lurking in the underbrush. Wait here. I'll tell you when it's safe to go on."

Garrid waved his wings to stretch them. "I'll do that, Li'l."

"Don't bother," said Li'l. "Even a bat like me can handle this."

"What was that supposed to mean?" he said, settling back on my shoulder as Li'l flew away. "She's not acting like herself at all. I wish I knew what was bothering her."

"That's a woman for you," said Eadric. "One little mistake and they're mad at you for days."

"What mistake? I don't even know what I did wrong!" wailed Garrid. "She was fine at the party last night. My relatives are all crazy about her."

When Li'l finally returned, we followed her through the trees to a patch of underbrush that had been trampled flat. The rotten-egg smell of troll was so strong that we had to hold our noses before we reached it and long after we'd passed by.

"I think we would have known they were here," I said.

"Anything with a nose would know they were here," said Eadric. "There's nothing subtle about trolls."

"The entrance is up ahead," said Li'l. "There are two trolls playing a game with bones just inside. You can't see them until you go in.'

"Sentries," said Eadric. "Ferdy and I'll take care of them."

"Save your blade," said Garrid. "There's no need to let the trolls know you're here if they don't already. I'll distract them and . . ."

"*We'll* distract them, you mean," Li'l said with a bite to her voice.

Garrid glanced at her, then nodded. "Li'l and I will distract them and let you know when you can come in. Be ready. This won't take long."

While Eadric and I hid among the boulders and loose rocks edging the entrance to the caves, Li'l and Garrid flew toward the opening, flitting around each other in what I would have thought was a friendly way if I hadn't been able to hear them.

"What other relatives haven't you told me about, Garrid?" asked Li'l. "Are your parents still alive, or any brothers or sisters?"

"I was an only child, Li'l. I told you that. And both of

my parents were killed in the vampire-werewolf wars. Why do you ask? Look, the trolls are behind that rock. The big hairy one has a club."

"I'm not stupid or blind. I can see them and they both have clubs," said Li'l. "I just wondered who else you hadn't told about me because you were too embarrassed. Ooh! Watch out! The hairy one almost got you!"

Garrid grunted, then said, "Embarrassed? Because of you? You can't possibly think that!" The vampire huffed, panting with exertion. "Take that! And that! Look out, Li'l! That one's going for his club!"

"Garrid, watch out! Garrid? Don't worry! I'm coming! Squeeze my mate, will you, you rotten, scum-sucking, dirt-licking . . . Ha! How'd you like that! Want another one? One good bite deserves another and . . . there! Good! Garrid, are you all right?"

"I'm fine! It takes more than a clout on the head and a ham-fisted squeeze to hurt me. Uh-oh. They're not giving up, Li'l. It looks as if a bat attack isn't enough to get rid of these dimwits. Watch out. I'm going to . . ."

"Garrid! Why'd you do that?" shrieked Li'l.

"Good day, gentlemen," Garrid said in his man voice. Although I couldn't see him, I knew he'd changed from a bat into his human-looking self. "I've never tasted troll blood before, but I like it now that I have. I'll give you a choice: which one of you wants to join us for all eternity and which one wants to die this very minute?"

166

"Aagh!" bellowed the two trolls, kicking up gravel as they ran past Eadric and me. I giggled when I saw that they kept their hands covering their beefy necks as they ran into the forest, because I could hear Garrid saying, "I knew they couldn't tell one of us from the other. Thank you for biting that one, Li'l. I couldn't bring myself to do it. Blood that foul would have curdled in my stomach and made me ill for days."

"The funny thing is that I couldn't actually bite him. His skin was too thick," said Li'l.

"Then his head must be thick, too," said Garrid. "Because he thought you had!"

"What happened to the trolls?" Eadric asked when I nudged him. "I couldn't hear a thing."

"They thought that Li'l and Garrid were vampires out for their blood," I said. "Let's go before the trolls stop running and decide to come back."

A bat once again, Garrid was waiting for us at the tunnel entrance. He must have heard what I'd told Eadric because he said, "They won't be back here any time soon. Li'l and I made a big impression."

"I wish I'd seen it," said Eadric.

"Maybe next time," said Garrid. "But only if Li'l . . . Where did she go? She can't be mad at me *again*!" Turning on a wing tip, he flew into the cave after his wife.

"He means she can't *still* be mad, doesn't he?" said Eadric.

"Now what did you mean when you accused me of being embarrassed?" I heard Garrid say to Li'l.

"What am I supposed to think when you don't introduce me to anyone? I didn't even know you had any living relatives until last night. It must be hard to say, 'I'd like you to meet my wife. She's a real bat.'"

"Don't be ridiculous!" said Garrid. "I love you. I'll announce it to the whole world if you want me to. World, this is my wife, Li'l. She's a real bat! See—I wasn't embarrassed at all."

"You wouldn't be—here inside a mountain where no one can hear you except me. And don't you dare tell me that my feelings are ridiculous. You have no right to . . ."

"Is everything all right?" Eadric asked, taking my hand in his. "You look worried."

"Everything is fine," I said, giving his hand a squeeze, but I was wondering if Eadric and I were going to argue like Li'l and Garrid once we were married.

Although we'd packed special torches to take into the caverns, we'd lost them along with everything else when we'd escaped the trolls at the river. Learning of this, Garrid had asked his relatives to make torches for us, something vampires rarely needed. We were happy enough to have them when we started out, but they soon became a nuisance, because they bled dark smoke that stank even more than the ever-present rotten-egg smell of the caves and were sure to give us away. When we came to a deserted sentry post in the tunnel and found some of the trolls' torches, we were delighted to exchange them for ours.

"At least these smell like the rest of the torches around here," Eadric said as he lit them.

"That's true," I said. "But don't you think it's odd that no one is here? Two tunnels merge at this very spot. It seems like an important place for a sentry."

"Maybe they're taking a dinner break," said Shelton, who was riding on my shoulder again. "I know I would if I could."

"And abandon their posts? A real soldier wouldn't do that," scoffed Eadric.

"These are trolls," I said. "Who knows what they do. Still, I think it's odd."

"Hmm," said Eadric, kneeling down to study the other objects the trolls had abandoned.

"There you are," sang out Li'l as she and Garrid flew into sight.

"There's another abandoned sentry post up ahead," said Garrid.

Lil flew closer, making her shadow loom large on the passage wall behind her. "What do you think it means?"

"I'm not sure," said Eadric. "It looks as if the trolls took off in a hurry, leaving nearly everything behind." He poked something with the toe of his boot, turning it over. "See, here's a club, and this was probably someone's meal." A bloody haunch of some kind of animal lay in the dust, covered with soft, wormlike insects.

"Keep your eyes open," said Garrid. "There's something strange about this. It isn't normal for trolls to abandon food."

"Maybe it's a trap," said Shelton. "Crabs know all about traps."

"Then why do so many get caught in them?" asked Eadric.

Shelton waved his eyestalks in irritation. "I said we know about them. That doesn't mean we understand them."

This time when Li'l and Garrid flew ahead, they waited for us at the next abandoned sentry post. Eadric found bone fragments like the ones the first trolls had been using to play a game as well as a note written in some strange lettering. "I might be able to read that," said Garrid. "You pick up all sorts of things when you live as long as I have. Let me see . . . Ah, yes. It says, 'Take two blister beetles and call me in the morning.'"

"It sounds like someone wasn't feeling well," I said.

"Maybe," said Eadric. "I just wish I knew what was going on."

Li'l and Garrid took off again, but were back a few minutes later with news to share. "There's a troll up ahead," said Li'l. "He's lying on the ground moaning."

We started to hurry. "Ferdy and I can get him to tell us what's going on," Eadric said, tapping his sword's hilt for emphasis.

"Don't take Ferdy out unless it's absolutely necessary," I told Eadric. "You know how loud he is."

Eadric looked annoyed. "He can be quiet when he has to be."

"Uh-huh," I said. "I've heard him hum. Just keep him in his scabbard if you can."

"Say," said Shelton. "You do know where you're going, don't you? There could be miles of passages in here. Do you know which one we want?"

"Of course we do," Eadric said, turning to me. "We do, don't we?"

I shook my head. "Not exactly. All I know is that he's being held in a room near the troll queen's treasure chamber."

"You mean we have to search this entire mountain?" asked Li'l.

I felt defensive when I said, "At least I picked the right mountain. This is where the trolls live, so he has to be around here somewhere."

"We'll find him," said Eadric. "We just have to start thinking like trolls."

"As long as you don't start acting like one," muttered Shelton.

"If anyone asked me," said Garrid, "I'd say that we're heading in the right direction. Li'l and I explored some of the side passages. Most of them looked like no one has set foot in there for years. The passage we're in is the most traveled. I think that if we look for the more heavily guarded passageways, we're bound to find him."

"You're so smart," Li'l told Garrid, gazing at him with love in her eyes. Apparently their conversation had taken a different turn when we could no longer hear them.

"Gick! Not you, too! It's bad enough when *they're* all mushy," Shelton said, pointing at Eadric and me. "I thought bats were smarter than that."

Eadric grinned. "I guess not."

Shelton almost fell off my shoulder when I jabbed Eadric in the side with my elbow.

We found the sick troll lying in the entrance to a large cavern. He was alone, although there were enough weapons and food scattered around him for two or three trolls. He moaned when he saw us, then fell back and closed his eyes. After glancing at me, Eadric approached the troll with his hand on Ferdy's hilt, but without pulling the sword from its scabbard. Keeping a cautious distance, he poked the troll with his foot, saying, "Sit up and answer some questions."

The troll rolled his head from side to side and moaned. "Go 'way," he mumbled. "Not want now. Eat later when feel better."

"I think he's sick," I said, going to stand beside Eadric. "Look at his face."

Blotchy and covered with deep purple spots, the troll did look terrible. He was sweating profusely, and his long dark hair was plastered to his head. Looking down from his perch on my shoulder, Shelton said, "That's a troll? They looked scarier at night."

The troll opened his eyes again, only this time his gaze fell on Shelton. "Ohhh, I seeing things," he moaned, and he covered his eyes with his hand. I'd never really noticed a troll's hands before. They were big and meaty with thick nails at least four inches long that looked like formidable weapons.

"Let's go," said Eadric. "We're not going to get anything out of him."

Although we kept to the most traveled passages, it was a while before we encountered any more trolls. We had passed through one cavern after another, all of them without sentries, when we came to an exceptionally large space where water covered most of the floor. Standing at its edge, it was impossible to tell how deep it was, but when we held up our torches, we could see sinuous shapes gliding along the bottom.

Eadric had warned everyone to be careful to avoid making noise that might echo, but Shelton was too excited at seeing so much water to keep quiet any longer. "Would you look at that!" he said, scrambling down from my shoulder to the ground. "A crab could enjoy a place like this!"

"Stay with us, Shelton!" I said.

My words bounced back, reminding me that I shouldn't have spoken. I was reaching to snatch the little crab from the water's edge when a voice croaked, "Who there?" from the far side of the pool. Shelton skittered away from my grasp as a torch flared, revealing a shaggy-headed troll. The troll must have been unsteady on his feet, because the torch dipped and swayed.

"Hurry!" Eadric said, turning to Garrid. "Stop that troll before he can raise an alarm."

Garrid darted over the water, turning into the shape of a man when he reached the other side. There was a shout and a splash, then the troll collapsed and Garrid was beckoning to us. Li'l had already joined him by then, so Eadric and I hurried around the pool.

"What did you do to him?" I asked Garrid. The troll lay sprawled on the ground, his arms thrown over his head.

"Nothing," said Garrid. "Look at his face."

I saw what he meant right away. The troll was sick, his face covered with purple spots just like the other troll we'd seen. His eyes were closed and his breathing was labored. He wasn't going to be warning anyone of anything for a while.

"What fell in the water?" Eadric asked, holding the torch out over the pool.

"He had a key in his hand and threw it in when he

174

saw me. I'm sorry I wasn't fast enough," Garrid said, shaking his head.

"A key to what?" I wondered aloud.

Garrid took the torch from Eadric and held it so that its light fell on the wall of the cavern where a metal-studded door blocked the passage. "I don't think he wanted us to open this," said Garrid. "Which means that it's probably the way we need to go."

Eadric crossed to the door and tried to open it. Nothing happened and he turned to face us, saying, "We need that key. Did anyone see where it went in?"

When no one had, Garrid held the torch over the pool so we could look for it. Li'l flew low over the water and was the first to spot the key resting on a yellow rock at the bottom. It was so far from the edge that someone was going to have to wade in to get it. Before Eadric could step into the pool, however, I knelt down beside it and reached my hand in to see how deep it was. The moment my fingers broke the surface, the water began to churn, and the fin of some sort of monster rose above the foam. I lurched backward, sitting down hard.

"What is that?" asked Li'l, frantically flapping her wings to get away from the water.

"Whatever it is, we can't go in," I told Eadric.

A round, scaly face surrounded by writhing tentacles

rose above the water, turning its catlike eyes on us. Its neck was long and slender like a snake, and as the water calmed, we could see the thickening of its body below it. Water bubbled at opposite sides of the pool. The monster wasn't alone.

"Clive," said the first monster. "Look at this!"

Another monster rose out of the water and swiveled its head to examine us. This monster didn't look anything like the first. It was all sharp angles and points with a narrow, pointed head, pointy, fan-shaped ears that stuck out to the sides, and a sharp crest that started just above its eyes and zigzagged down its back.

"They funny-looking trolls," said Clive.

A shapeless, jellylike sack that was mostly transparent floated across the water, rising and falling as it gulped or expelled air. While its friends talked, it raised a cluster of eyestalks from one of its bulges and waved them in our direction. "They not trolls," burbled the monster.

"What else they be, Edgar?" said the first monster.

"Don't know," said Edgar. "Look tasty, though."

"If not trolls, maybe can eat them," said Clive. "What you think, Churtle? Fatlippia make us promise not eat trolls, but she not say about those things."

"Can eat them, if not trolls," said Churtle, the first monster.

I took Eadric aside and said, "No one is going in after that key. Do you think we can talk them into giving it to us?"

"Perhaps they'll do it if we give them something in return," Eadric said, scratching his chin.

"That rude, talking secretlike," said Clive.

"Maybe are trolls," burbled Edgar. "Trolls always rude."

"What could we possibly have that they would want?" I asked Eadric, trying to keep my voice soft enough that the monsters couldn't hear me.

"That's a good point," said Eadric. "Could you use your magic here? I remember how good you were at taking care of the monsters Grassina put in the moat during her nasty days."

I shook my head. "We're in the troll queen's own mountain, at her very doorstep. Using magic now would be like knocking on the door to announce that we're here. This is no place for magic! No, we're going to have to think of something else."

"We ask them," said Clive. "They know if trolls or not."

"Is there anything I can do to help?" Li'l asked, landing on my shoulder.

"I'll do whatever I can," said Garrid. "But I must warn you that I don't know how to swim."

"Then I'm the best swimmer here," said Eadric. "If you three could distract them, maybe I could slip into the water and . . ."

"Get eaten?" I said, hating the idea. "I'd use magic before I'd let you do that."

"Hey you! You trolls?" called Clive. "You tell us. We hungry. You look yummy."

"Pretend you don't understand what they're saying," I whispered to my friends.

"We hear you!" said Churtle. "Why trolls pretend can't understand?"

"Maybe proves them not trolls," said Clive.

"But can understand, so must be trolls," said Churtle.

"This too hard," moaned Edgar. "Edgar not understand."

"Hey!" said Clive. "What that? Something move at bottom."

"I not see anything," said Churtle. "Maybe piece of Edgar. Edgar, you lose piece again? Pull self together. Churtle hate when Edgar let self go."

"It not Edgar!" said Edgar, sounding as if his feelings had been hurt. "Edgar all here."

"How you tell?" said Clive. "Clive not know where Edgar is until swim into Edgar. It disgusting!"

"Edgar not disgusting! Clive disgusting! Clive poke Edgar for fun! Laugh when Edgar leak. Clive mean. Edgar not like Clive." Raising one of his jellylike bulges out of the water, Edgar swatted Clive on his snout.

Clive spluttered and coughed, then said, "Edgar runny glob of snot! I not like Edgar either. See how Edgar like be poked." His crest rose as Clive lunged for Edgar. The jellylike monster gave a high-pitched shriek as he let all his air out at once, sinking to the bottom like a stone. Clive followed, appearing to shrink as he swam farther and farther down.

"Must see this! Wait for Churtle!" shouted Churtle. He plunged into the water, his smooth back arching above the surface, then disappeared with a flick of his tail flukes.

"Yoo-hoo, over here! Is this what you were looking for?" It was Shelton, holding the key with both front claws.

"You got it!" I said, reaching down to pick up the little crab.

"Here, you take it," he said, dropping it into my hand. "That thing is heavy!"

"When you ran off that way, I thought we'd lost you for good," I said.

"Naw, I just wanted to wet my shell. But I don't like that water. Tastes funny. Too many minerals, I guess. So," he said, his eyestalks perking up. "Anything interesting happen while I was gone?"

Twelve

I held my breath as Eadric put the key in the lock and didn't exhale until he'd pushed the door open. Li'l fluttered beside me, too nervous to hold still. We were both disappointed when the passage beyond didn't look like anything special. Then Garrid stepped over the threshold and raised the torch high. "Oh," we breathed, for the stone walls were studded with gems of every color. Although the light from the torch wasn't very bright, it reflected off the gems, making them sparkle and wink until our eyes ached and we had to look away.

"This is the passage I saw in my farseeing ball," I said. "They took Bradston this way."

"No wonder they keep that door locked," said Shelton. "I wonder how hard it would be to pry off those stones. I bet Coral would like one!"

"We're not thieves," said Eadric. "We're here to get my brother back and nothing more."

"Spoilsport," grumbled Shelton. Before I could stop

him, he'd scrambled from my shoulder to the ground and was poking at one of the gems. I was surprised when he snapped it off with his claw. "Did you see that?" asked Shelton. "They were stuck on. Someone put them there to make the walls look pretty."

"And it worked, too," said Li'l. "This is beautiful." I saw the way Garrid was watching her when she said that and wondered how long it would be before he gave her a gem of some kind.

We knew we were getting close to the queen's chamber when we came to the next door. It was more ornate than the first, with crudely printed letters that Garrid told us meant, "Keep out! This means you, Dunderhead!" It was obvious that the sentry had left in a hurry. Not only had he forgotten his club, but he had shut the door without making sure that it had actually closed. When Eadric set his hand on it, the door creaked open.

The room beyond was as unexpected as the gem-decorated passage had been. It was draped in fabrics of garishly bright oranges, pinks, purples, and reds that covered the stone walls so that it seemed more like a tent than a cave. Equally bright carpets had been scattered across the uneven floor, hiding holes and bumps and making walking difficult. Here and there matching pillows were mounded in piles like the leavings of some outrageously colored beast. Even with all the fabric, the room was chilly and damp and smelled strongly of mildew as well as rotten eggs.

I saw cracked urns overflowing with the feathers of exotic birds, and benches made of bone and antlers with the skulls still attached. A dainty table of tarnished silver held drinking vessels of all sorts, from rude clay mugs to finely wrought chalices made of gold. Whereas some held the dregs of a dark liquid, others held only dust.

I was walking toward the table when I nearly kicked over a basket of fruit that had been left on the floor beside one of the mounds of pillows. The grapes were withered, the apples brown and mushy, the rest so rotted that I couldn't tell what they were. When I tried to go around the basket, my foot slipped into a hole under the carpet and I stumbled, landing on my knees. I started to push myself up and found that I was looking into the glazed-over eyes of a troll. I recognized her at once. It was the troll queen, and she didn't look at all well.

I stood up and retreated a pace. The troll queen lay sprawled on her back behind the pile of pillows. All four of her heads were soaked with sweat and had tangled hair and cracked lips. Dark purple spots made random patterns on her faces. Although the head with the long brunette hair appeared to be asleep, the head next to it was delirious, turning from side to side and mumbling, "Too many birds in pie," and "Rampaging better in winter." Even though misery had distorted her face, I recognized her as the red-haired head who had threatened me over my farseeing ball.

I was startled when the head with reddish, light brown hair blinked and stared at me with wary eyes. "You here," she said, her hoarse voice almost too faint to hear. "Army searching river. Move on, we say. She not there anymore. We knew you come. He said so."

"Who said I'd come?" I asked, bending down to hear her better.

A head with strawberry blonde hair stared at me through eyes as big as cartwheels. "What she do, Grunella?" she asked with a catch in her voice. "She want hurt us? Wish Fatlippia awake. Ingabinga all right?"

"Quiet, Tizzy!" barked the head named Grunella. "No start crying. I not know what human do now."

"Emma, what did you find?" asked Eadric from across the room.

Li'l fluttered toward me, making funny little sounds when she saw the troll queen. "She found her! Emma found the queen!"

"For goodness' sake, get away from her!" Eadric exclaimed as he jumped over a pile of pillows and staggered across the uneven floor.

The troll queen's hand shook, and her fist started to clench. Then it went limp and Grunella groaned. "I not move stupid thing. Not since Fatlippia start raving." She nodded toward the delirious head next to her. "Wake up, Fatlippia! Company here!"

"Fish follow Fatlippia home, so I . . ."

"Fatlippia, wake up! Need control hand!"

"Name him Scales. That good name, you not think?"

"Fatlippia! Need hand to . . . Oh, you no help." The head twisted aside and spat at the wall, then turned back to look at me. "You be happy Fatlippia sick. If she awake instead of Grunella, Fatlippia find way stop you. You kill us now and steal treasures?"

"No," I said. "We never intended to hurt you. We just want Bradston back along with your promise that you'll leave him alone."

One side of her mouth quirked in a half smile. "Give you word, but not do any good. Smart troll never keep promises. Promises for weak soft-skins. But I not want him. He more trouble than worth. You tell him Grunella say so."

"Say," said Garrid. "Look at this. What do you suppose it's for?"

I had to stand to see what he was holding. When I realized what it was, I nearly broke my neck tripping over the basket of fruit as I ran to take it from him. I hadn't wanted to let Eadric know how worried I was about the magic-seeing ball, but if this was actually it . . . "Let me see that," I said, snatching the gray-green ball from his hands. I carried it back to where the troll queen lay and held it up for her to see. "This is what you used to see me when I did magic, isn't it?"

Grunella glanced at the ball, then looked away, but

184

the flicker of recognition I saw in her eyes was almost enough. Almost, but not quite. "We'll just see then, won't we?" I said. Raising the ball so everyone could see it, I made up a small spell on the spot. It felt wonderful to use my magic again!

> Make this chamber smell like flowers.
> Make the smell stay here for hours.

And just like that, the odor of mildew and rotten eggs was gone and the room smelled like a heady bouquet of roses and lilacs and the lilies my mother had had planted all around the moat. I was watching the ball the whole time, so I saw when it clouded over and a tiny version of me appeared standing in the troll queen's room.

"Pew!" said Grunella. "What that stench?"

"It's how your world smells right before this thing is destroyed," I said, heading toward the door. "Excuse me, everyone. I'll be back in a minute."

I hated that someone had made a magic-seeing ball that was focused on me and would know whenever I used my magic. Rather than have it fall into someone else's hands, I was going to do whatever it took to destroy it. The ball was heavy and hard to break, but I threw it against the wall until it split. I bent down to pick up the pieces and found an auburn hair the same color as mine stuck to the inside of a larger fragment. "That's odd," I

185

muttered, then remembered that whoever had made it had to have something of mine to focus it. The hair didn't just look like mine; it *was* mine. Whoever had made the magic-seeing ball must have been close to me at some point, or at least knew someone who had been. Jorge had been in our castle, although he was in our dungeon the entire time. I had never gone to see him, but it was possible that someone had given the hair to him. Thinking about his room and the furniture he'd been using, it was even possible that he'd gotten it off my old bed.

After stuffing the hair into the pouch I wear at my side, I smashed the pieces until they were small enough that I could grind them under my heel. Once I was finished, I felt much better.

When I returned to the troll queen's chamber, Tizzy was pouting. "Why you do that? Tizzy thought ball pretty."

Grunella sighed. "You happy now?" she asked me.

"Not yet," I said. "Tell me—how many of those were there?"

"Grunella not tell you!" said the head.

"Why you ask?" said Tizzy. "You want break other one, too?"

"Tizzy!" wailed Grunella. "Now she know is other one!"

"Thank you," I said. "I don't suppose you'd care to tell us where we can find Bradston?"

"Not in million years," Grunella said, chortling.

"She not staying that long, right, Grunella?" asked Tizzy.

"Prince Eadric, over here!" said Garrid. "Li'l found a door behind the cloth. If someone can hold the cloth aside . . ."

"Uh-oh," said Tizzy. "They find it!"

Grunella glared at the other head. "Tizzy! You not talk anymore!"

"Let me help," said Eadric. Grabbing a fistful of the fabric, he tore it from the wall, exposing a door that was as short and wide as a troll. It groaned like one, too, when Eadric forced it open. The room beyond was dark, the torches lighting it having fizzled out. I peered around Garrid and Eadric as they bent down to enter the room, taking our torch with them. It was the same room that Eadric and I had seen in the banshee's mirror.

Only a few paces inside the door Bradston lay on the floor, his head pillowed on his arms. The two trolls we'd seen in the mirror lay side by side in the corner, their faces spotted, their breathing loud and nasal. "Bradston!" Eadric said, his brother's name catching in his throat. "Poor little guy! What have they done to you?" The boy's face was dotted with scabs, but otherwise he looked fine to me.

"Uh, Eadric," I began.

"They must have infected him with their horrible

187

disease," said Eadric, shaking his head. "Look at his face! Who knows what this is going to do to him."

"Not much, once the scabs heal," I said. "Eadric, your brother was sick first. Your mother didn't tell us what he had, but it looks like it was chicken pox. I had it when I was five. Aside from a scar on my arm where I picked off a scab, I was fine. He will be, too, but I'm not so sure about those trolls. I don't think they gave it to him. I think he gave it to them."

"That can't be. Look at how still he is. Bradston, wake up. It's me, Eadric. We're here to rescue you. Did you see that?" he said, turning to me. "He doesn't respond. I'm sure there's something seriously wrong with him." I sighed and shook my head, but Eadric was adamant. "You wouldn't understand. You've never had a little brother."

Kneeling on the floor beside his brother's inert body, Eadric bent down to scoop the boy into his arms, and got clonked soundly on his nose when Bradston sat up with a start.

"Ow!" howled Eadric, holding his hand to his nose. Blood was already seeping between his fingers when Bradston looked up and laughed. "That was a good one! I got three trolls that way, and now you!"

"You little monster!" said Eadric.

"Why'd you bring her with you?" Bradston asked, looking at me. "Mother calls her the nasty little witch who cast a love spell on you. Is it true?"

"Of course not," I said indignantly. "I never cast a love spell on Eadric."

"I meant the nasty little witch part," said Bradston. "She said a lot of other things, too. Want to hear what they were?"

"No!" Eadric and I said in unison.

Bradston stood up and stretched. "So, you came to get me out or what? You sure took your time. Do you know how awful it's been? There's nothing to do here. Trolls have to be the stupidest people in the world. Say, you didn't bring something to eat, did you? I'm starved."

"He talk too much," called Grunella from the other room.

I saw a satisfied smile flicker on Bradston's lips and shuddered, feeling a rush of sympathy for the trolls.

We were back in the troll queen's chamber when Bradston noticed Li'l. "Am I the only one who saw that there's a bat in here? Give me a rock and I'll kill it."

"You'll do no such thing!" I said. "You stay away from her! That bat happens to be one of my best friends."

"That figures," said Bradston. "A witch and her bat. I bet you're really an old woman who drinks bat juice or something to stay young. I bet you're a whole lot older than you look."

"Bradston, that's enough," growled Eadric. "And to think that my mother dotes on him."

189

"Does she know he acts like this?" I asked.

Eadric shook his head. "She hasn't the least idea. He acts like an angel when she's watching."

"I can silence him for you if you'd like me to, Emma," offered Garrid.

Bradston stuck out his tongue at Garrid, then turned to me and smirked.

Eadric sighed. "Please forgive him. He's ill and doesn't know what he's saying."

"He's not that ill," I said. "And he knows exactly what he's saying."

"My parents are never going to let you marry him," the boy said. "I heard them talking. They're going to send Eadric far away and see that he gets engaged to some other princess. They said that anyone would make him a better wife than you would."

"I should turn him over my knee," said Eadric.

"Don't bother," I said, having had enough of Eadric's younger brother. "I have a better idea. Why don't we just turn him over to your mother? I think they deserve each other."

Choosing one of the cleaner rugs on the troll queen's floor, I said a quick spell to enable it to fly. Bradston was eager to take his seat beside Eadric, and even let his big brother put his arm around his shoulders to keep him safe. With Garrid seated beside me and Li'l cradled in his hands, I made the carpet rise before saying,

Take us to the young lad's mother.
She awaits his quick return.
Keep him there until he grows up.
He still has so much to learn.

Never more than five or six feet
Should this wayward youngster stray.
By his mother's side he'll linger
Till his twenty-first birthday.

"Does that mean what I think it does?" Eadric asked as a breeze sprang up around us.

"Yes," I said. "Bradston is going to be a real mama's boy."

Thirteen

"That was the best thing I've ever done!" exclaimed Bradston as the carpet settled to the floor of Queen Frazzela's solarium. "It was even better than stealing eagles' eggs or dumping trash over the parapets onto people! Give me the rug. I can think of all sorts of places I'd like to go."

"Really?" I said. "That's funny, because I can think of a lot of places that I'd like to send you. I'm not going to give you a magic carpet, though." Although the carpet was resting on the floor, a ripple ran through it every few seconds as if it wanted to fly away. Certain that the boy would try to take it when I wasn't around to stop him, I said a quick spell to turn the carpet back into an ordinary rug. It went limp with a soft, breathy sigh.

"Why'd you do that?" squeaked the boy. "You're mean! If you don't make it fly again, I'll tell my mother that you did and then . . ."

"Oh, look, there's your mother now!" I said, gesturing

behind him. "I'm sure she'd be very interested in what-ever you have to say."

Queen Frazzela sat open-mouthed, making funny little gurgling sounds. We'd flown through her solarium window, landing between her and a group of ladies. One of the ladies fainted when she saw us, and most of the rest just looked dumbfounded. At a word from Queen Frazzela, the other ladies-in-waiting helped their friend from the room, leaving three other women behind. My grandmother Olivene and my aunt Grassina looked de-lighted to see me. My mother looked perturbed.

"Bradston, is that really you?" said his mother.

The boy didn't look happy, but I didn't know if it was because I'd denied him something he wanted or because he'd said some things in front of his mother that he'd rather she hadn't heard. He covered it well, however, forc-ing tears to come to his eyes and throwing himself into his mother's arms. "Oh, Mama," he said. "It was awful!"

Queen Frazzela drew him into her arms and kissed the top of his head. "My poor little darling," she said, rocking him back and forth as if he were a baby. She was cooing and patting his back when he peeked over her shoulder and gave me a sly look of triumph.

Just wait, I thought, remembering my spell.

"My poor boy! Thank goodness you're all right. Those horrible trolls. You must have been terrified. And I bet you didn't sleep a wink." She turned to my relatives, saying, "Bradston needs his rest. He's been through a terrible ordeal. You'll have to excuse me. . . ."

"Of course, my dear," said Olivene, giving mother and son a sympathetic smile. Bradston was walking dutifully beside his mother when he looked back and stuck out his tongue. Grassina looked surprised, but Olivene just smiled all the more widely and winked at me.

As soon as Frazzela and Bradston were gone, Garrid cleared his throat and said, "Eadric, Li'l and I need to take naps. If you could suggest somewhere quiet and dark . . ."

"You'd probably like the top room in the old tower. No one goes there anymore."

"Perfect," said Garrid.

When Garrid left the room with Li'l on his shoulder, he still looked like a man. Then a whiff of something cold and dank drifted in from the hall, and I knew that he hadn't waited long before turning into a bat.

"It's good to see you both safe and sound," said my mother. "Queen Frazzela told me that the trolls had killed you, but Olivene and Grassina assured me that you were unhurt. I've never known them to be wrong."

I glanced at where they sat side by side on a bench in the sunlight. Grassina smiled and tapped the farseeing ball she wore on a chain around her neck.

"Why didn't your mother thank you after you rescued Bradston?" my mother asked Eadric.

"She doesn't like magic," he replied.

"Neither do I, but I appreciate what it can do for us and know enough to respect it. Apparently your mother does not."

"I'm afraid her attitude is common in this kingdom, Mother," I said.

"Then I fear for your mother and your people, Eadric," she said. "And my respect for both has been woefully diminished."

"We knew there was something wrong with Frazzela when she came to the tournament," said my grandmother. "Your mother was so rude to our Emma."

"I remember," said Eadric. "I've already spoken to her about it."

"Tell us what happened after the army ran back here with their tails between their legs," said Grassina. "I saw them coming in my farseeing ball. I think I've spent more time looking into it these past few days than all the other times I've used it put together."

"We were preparing to follow you when I asked Grassina to see how you were doing," said my mother. "She saw that something had gone amiss, although she couldn't tell what. Her reports were so confusing: you were safe, you were in danger, you were fine . . . We stopped only three times on our way here. I've never felt so rushed in my life. When she saw you enter that mountain, your father almost set out after you, but Grassina still insisted that everything was all right."

"And it was, wasn't it?" said Grassina. "Tell me about the cockatrices. I want to hear how you got out of that one."

"And the banshee," said Grandmother. "Don't forget about her."

My mother stood and straightened her skirts around her. "If you're going to talk about such things, I might as well leave. Although I must say I was delighted when Grassina reported that you were able to accomplish so much without using magic for a change, Emma. I'm . . . proud of you," she said, sounding as if she'd surprised even herself. Gathering her embroidery, she started for the door, pausing on her way out to say, "That young man with the bat looked familiar. Have I met him before?"

"At Father's tournament," I said. "Did Father accompany you here?"

"Yes, and so did Haywood," said my grandmother. "We arrived yesterday."

"About that young man who came with you," said Mother. "Why would he want to sleep in a tower? Wouldn't he prefer to have a room?"

"He doesn't need one," said Eadric.

"Oh," my mother said, the muscles around her eyes and mouth tightening. "Don't tell me any more. I'm sure it's something that I'd rather not know anything about. Mother, Grassina, I'll see you at supper. I believe that I'll go for a walk in the garden. I trust that no one will be discussing magic there."

"Now," said Grassina after my mother had gone. "We want to hear everything. Start with how the trolls attacked in the middle of the night."

So Eadric and I told them about the trolls and the devices they'd used to sense my magic. Although I'd smashed the queen's magic-seeing ball, her army must still have theirs. I put finding it on my mental list of things I had to do.

We told them about the sea monsters and the cockatrices. Grassina said that she might like to turn into a weasel and hunt cockatrices someday. We told them about the banshee and the vampires. Olivene wondered if the banshee knew an old acquaintance of hers—someone she'd met when she was under the family curse.

They were particularly interested in the troll queen's mountain and its tunnels and caverns. Olivene and Grassina told us that the monsters sounded familiar. When we told them about the sick trolls, they said that it sounded as if they had troll pox, a nasty yet rarely fatal disease. We were still discussing the pox when Queen Frazzela returned with Bradston in tow.

"I thought the boy was going to rest," said my grandmother.

Bradston's expression was sour, and I could tell he wasn't happy to be back with us.

197

"He refuses to leave my side," said Queen Frazzela. "I tucked him into bed, but he jumped out and followed me when I left. The experience with the trolls must have been too much for the poor child." She patted his head, then leaned down to kiss him on the cheek, not noticing his pained expression.

I was trying not to smile when my eyes met my grandmother's. She winked at me and I had to look away.

"It occurred to me that I've been remiss," Queen Frazzela told Eadric. "I should have thanked you for what you've done. You brought my baby back to me when I thought he was gone forever. I've never heard of anyone getting a child back whom the trolls had taken. Thank you, Eadric."

"And Emma," Eadric said, giving my hand a squeeze.

Queen Frazzela sighed. "And Emma. I must admit, I never thought I'd say this, but after what Bradston told me, I, well . . ."

"Can see how magic might be useful at times?" said Eadric.

"Yes, exactly!" The queen looked relieved that she hadn't had to say it herself.

"And it might be handy to have a witch in the family?" Eadric continued.

"I never said . . . but I suppose . . . well, yes, that, too."

"I'm curious," said my grandmother. "What did Bradston tell you, exactly?"

"He told me about the trolls, of course. They were horrible to him. And he told me about the dangerous passages and the cave where he was held prisoner and the horrid monsters he saw." The queen dabbed at her eyes with a cloth she pulled from her sleeve. "When I think about what my poor boy had to endure . . . Thank you for getting him out of there!" she said, and this time she looked straight at me.

Bradston looked disgruntled. I was convinced that he'd probably described his plight to his mother to gain more sympathy, not so she could picture what we had gone through to get him out. He kicked at an uneven spot on the floor, looking as if he'd rather be anywhere else but there, yet he stayed by his mother's side when she collected her embroidery and sat down.

Eadric yawned, exaggerating it until his mother couldn't help but notice. "I need a nap," he said.

"So do I," I said, following his lead.

"There will be a feast tonight," said Queen Frazzela. "In honor of Bradston's safe return."

"Good," said Eadric, yawning again for real. "We'll be there."

Supper was hours away, however, and we were too hungry to wait. Eadric was showing me the way to the kitchen when we ran into his father in the Great Hall. "Eadric, my boy! I knew you could do it! Congratulations! Into the trolls' mountain and out again safe and sound. It's an extraordinary accomplishment. You'll have to tell me how you managed it. A little magical help from your Emma, I presume. I must say, after everything that has happened over the past few days, my opinion of magic has changed. I've never really understood it, but then maybe it has its place whether you understand it or not. It certainly saved the day this time. I heard all about the trolls attacking and how you kept the bulk of their army off my men with that thing you did to the stream, Emma. I wish I had someone like you attached to my army!" King Bodamin winked at me, and I could see that Eadric was as surprised as I was.

"We're grateful, the queen and I, although she might not know how to say it. She dotes on that young scamp. I'll have to give him a talking-to when he's feeling fit again. Shouldn't have gone off like that. Not with trolls and who knows what else outside the castle walls. We'll have to see that he doesn't stray again. Assign him his own guard perhaps."

"That won't be necessary," I told him. "I don't think he'll go far from his mother now."

"Good, good," the king said, beaming. "We can't have this sort of thing happening again. It caused quite an uproar, didn't it? Why, I was telling King Limelyn . . . You do know that your parents are here, don't you, m'dear? They arrived yesterday along with so many carts and carriages that . . . Well, I'm sure you understand."

Eadric had waited until his father paused to take a

breath. "If you'll excuse us, Father, we were on our way to get something to eat."

"Quite right, Eadric. Quite right. You must be starved. Come see me after you've eaten."

"I will, Father. We have a lot to talk about," Eadric said, giving me a meaningful glance.

His father nodded, saying, "Indeed we do, my boy. Indeed we do! Now, don't eat too much. I understand that there's to be a special supper tonight. Make sure you save room for the stewed eels. They're my favorite."

It didn't take us long to get a bite to eat. The kitchen staff fawned over Eadric, congratulating him and offering him the best cuts of leftover roasts and the freshest fruit. They smiled at me, a big difference from the disapproving looks I'd gotten from the residents of the castle a few days earlier.

When we'd finished eating, we left the kitchen and were crossing the Great Hall when my father hailed me. "My darling Emma, how are you?"

"Better," I replied without explaining that it was because I could use my magic again.

He nodded as if he understood. "Please join me for a moment," he said, and he led us to a bench away from the bustle of the Hall.

Eadric put his arm around me as we sat, pulling me close to his side. My father cleared his throat and said, "King Bodamin and I have agreed that there's no reason to put off your marriage any longer. You two make a perfect match and will unite our kingdoms in a way that would benefit both. As I have no other heirs, Emma will be queen of Greater Greensward one day. Bodamin assures me that Eadric will rule Upper Montevista. Eadric, you have shown great strength of character and bravery, two qualities that your father had hoped to see in his heir. There's no reason you can't rule both countries side by side. I must admit, I'd thought Bodamin was against the marriage, but I was surprised by how quickly he agreed to it. He mentioned something about family members helping his army. I didn't quite follow that, but he might have been alluding to the way you took care of the trolls."

"So he gave his permission?" I said, not quite believing what I thought I'd heard.

My father nodded. "The wedding will be tomorrow. Everyone we would have wanted here for the wedding is already at the castle, although I daresay that Chartreuse and Frazzela will have others they want to invite. Bodamin and I will see that the appropriate documents are drawn up. He sent word to the local priest right after we spoke. Ah, there's your mother now. She's handling the rest of the arrangements."

I was stunned. I'd been afraid that we'd never get the approval of Eadric's parents, and now we were having the wedding the next day. I didn't know if I should be happy and excited, or frightened and tell them to wait because I wasn't ready. I would have liked to discuss it with Eadric, but he took off when we saw my mother bearing down on us with a determined look in her eyes.

"Did your father tell you about the wedding?" she asked me as Eadric hurried away.

I turned to my father, but he had already retreated across the Hall. "Yes, he did," I said. "Don't you think tomorrow is a little soon?"

"Of course I do, but the men have made up their minds. I'm determined to make the best of things, however, and you should, too. Although I may not have long to make the arrangements, I'm going to see that this wedding is done right, not like your aunt Grassina's. Now come with me. I have Maude waiting to start on your gown, and Frazzela has sent both of her seamstresses to assist. This shouldn't take long with three pairs of hands working on it."

I shouldn't have been surprised that Mother had brought her favorite seamstress with her from home. She usually traveled with a full entourage, just in case she needed someone's special talents. I followed her up the stairs reluctantly, unable to think of any plausible reason to get out of it.

Maude was very businesslike when we stepped into Queen Frazzela's solarium, as were the two older women helping her. They were finishing the last of my measurements when Queen Frazzela came to the door. I could hear her arguing with my mother from where I stood in the middle of the room, so I was curious when my mother came back alone.

"What was that all about?" I asked.

"Nothing really," said my mother. "Frazzela wanted to see what fabric you've chosen, but I told her she couldn't come in. She had Bradston with her and he refused to stay outside. That boy has become so insecure since you brought him home. He hasn't left his mother's side yet."

"That's odd," I said, pretending to watch the seamstress.

"She did tell me that she has the wedding feast well under control. She also said that the guests have begun to arrive. Those friends of yours, Oculura and Dyspepsia, are here. Your grandmother insisted that she be in charge of the invitations."

"What is Grassina doing?" I asked.

"She's taking care of the flowers. I just hope they aren't like the ones she had at her own wedding."

When the initial fittings were done, the seamstresses said I could go but had to return when they sent for me. They seemed smug in their ability to tell me what to do, even if it was for a short time, but I was happy just to have gotten my freedom back long enough to go see what was going on.

I was on my way to the Great Hall when I saw Eadric

very briefly. He was going to his own fittings, but was so nervous that he couldn't stand still and paced the whole time I was talking to him. "So the wedding is tomorrow," he said.

"Can you believe it? I didn't know what to say when Father told us."

"Are you all right with it being so soon? I don't want you to feel rushed."

I smiled, warmed by his concern. "I think it's wonderful," I said, realizing that I really did.

"It looks as if we have enough people to help out," he said, gesturing toward my aunt, who was bustling through the hall with an armload of ferns.

"Mmm hmm," I replied. "I just wonder whom my grandmother is inviting."

"I saw her waiting by the drawbridge. She seemed to be expecting someone."

"Dyspepsia and Oculura are already here. I think I'll go talk to Grandmother," I said, "and find out exactly who's on her list."

I didn't have to go far to find her. Some of her friends from the Old Witches' Retirement Community had arrived, and she was escorting them across the courtyard. After they'd offered me their congratulations, Grandmother sent them inside while we talked.

"Who else did you invite?" I asked.

"Grassina helped me with the list. We invited Pearl

and Coral, but Coral is still visiting her friends and Pearl has gone to see her sisters. I thought about inviting that little dragon friend of yours along with his parents until Grassina pointed out that Bodamin and Frazzela might not appreciate having three dragons in their castle."

"So who is coming?" I asked.

"We've invited all the fairies from Greater Greensward and Upper Montevista. I made sure that we didn't leave anyone out. You know how irate fairies can be if they think they've been slighted."

"Oh dear. I didn't think of them. We needed to invite the fairies, of course, but we'll have to make sure that everyone is extra nice to them, even the more peculiar ones. The last thing we need is another curse cast on the family. I'll explain it to Queen Frazzela and King Bodamin so they can tell everyone else."

"Good," said Grandmother. "It will be for only one day. Fairies don't like spending the night away from their own homes."

My search for the king and queen took me to the courtyard and all the public rooms, but it wasn't until I started asking if anyone had seen them that a maid said they were in the family corridor. I found them talking to Bradston outside the room where Eadric was getting fitted for his clothes.

". . . just for a little while," said the queen. "You're

perfectly safe here. No trolls will ever get into the castle. There's nothing to fear from . . ."

"I'm not afraid," Bradston said, looking more irritated than frightened.

The king threw up his hands. "Then why can't you stay in your room without your mother? You're too old to be following her everywhere. You haven't left her side since you came home. The poor woman can't even use the garderobe without you waiting for her on the other side of the door."

"Don't you think I'd like to stop following her?" said Bradston. "I just can't, that's all, and don't ask me why because I don't know the answer."

I'd been standing in the hall, wondering if I should leave and come back later, when Queen Frazzela glanced up and saw me. "Bodamin," she said, tilting her head in my direction.

The king turned to me, smiling. "Ah, there you are, my dear. All set for the big day tomorrow?"

"I'm sorry to interrupt, but that's what I wanted to talk about. I guess it's a good thing that I found all three of you together. We have some guests coming tomorrow who are a little unusual. Some are from Greater Greensward and some are from Upper Montevista. They're very sensitive, you see, and . . ."

"They're witches, I suppose," said Queen Frazzela.

207

"I should have known you'd open my home to the worst sort of people."

I took a deep breath, trying to keep myself calm. "They aren't witches, although we did invite a few, and I expect them to be treated with as much courtesy as any other guests," I said, looking straight at the queen. "The people I'm talking about are fairies. We invited them because they would have been insulted if we hadn't, which wouldn't bode well for either kingdom."

Bradston snickered. "You're going to have little fairies at your wedding? That's the stupidest thing I've ever heard!"

"Then listen to me, Bradston," I said, barely controlling my temper. "The stupidest thing would be if someone were to insult one of these fairies. They're very powerful and could make you miserable for the rest of your life if you so much as look at one of them in a funny way."

"I'm not surprised that you consort with fairies in your kingdom, but it's unheard of in Upper Montevista," the queen said in a voice I'm sure she thought sounded superior.

"I wouldn't say that exactly, my dear," said the king, rubbing his chin with his thumb and forefinger. "My father's older brother had some fairy friends. One day he told my father that he had fallen in love with a fairy lass and was going to attend one of their dances. He disappeared that night and no one ever heard from him again."

"Your mother told me that he died very young and that that's why your father inherited the throne," said the queen.

"My mother didn't want people to know what had really happened. I'm sure that most of the stories she told you were altered to fit her version of the truth. She refused to let anyone tell me fairy tales when I was growing up. She'd say that they were all lies, then check the doors and windows as if she feared that someone might have heard her."

"She was right to be afraid," I said. "If any fairies had, they might have taken offense. It's a mistake to ignore fairies, but it's an even bigger mistake to be rude or unkind toward them."

Bradston snorted as if he thought I was making it up, but King Bodamin looked thoughtful when he said, "You say the fairies who live in my kingdom are coming here tomorrow? How many should we expect?"

I shrugged. "I'm not sure. My grandmother might know."

The king nodded and looked at his son. "Bradston, I order you to be respectful toward all our guests. None of your tricks, understand?"

The boy hesitated as if he wanted to make a snide remark, then seemed to think better of it and said, "Yes, sir. If *you* say so." His parents were both looking my way when Bradston stuck out his tongue at me.

"I'll see that this gets relayed to the rest of the castle. Frazzela," the king said, turning to his wife, "regardless of your feelings, you're to treat them as honored guests."

The queen glared at me. "We would never have had to worry about any of this if Eadric had chosen a normal princess."

"Oh really?" I said. "And would that be a princess who had slept for a hundred years or one who cleaned house until her fairy godmother helped her go to a ball? I don't know about you, but I'm not sure I've ever met a normal princess."

King Bodamin chuckled. "She's got you there," he said to his wife. "It doesn't matter whether they should have been invited or not. They have been, so we'll do as Emma has asked. This should be interesting. I've always wanted to meet a fairy."

Wonderful, I thought, heading back to the Great Hall. *With Frazzela and Bradston around, something is bound to happen.* I began to wonder if my family was doomed to end one curse just to fall prey to another.

Fourteen

When I couldn't find Eadric, I decided to take a nap before I had to face everyone again at supper. The chamber I'd used before was just as I'd left it, which meant that the person who usually slept there had not come back. Because I didn't want to be disturbed, I said a spell to lock the door, and another to keep any outside noise from getting in, then lay on the bed and closed my eyes. I was almost asleep when I remembered what the troll queen had said. Although I'd asked her whom she meant when she told me, "He said you would come," we'd been interrupted before she answered, and I'd forgotten to ask her again. *Whom did she mean?* I wondered as I drifted off. *Why were they talking about me?*

I was exhausted and slept through supper and on into the night. It was midmorning when I woke again, feeling more refreshed than I had since leaving Greater Greensward. My grandmother was sitting at a table across from the stairwell waiting for me when I went downstairs.

"Come sit down," she said, waving me over. "I'll fill you in before your mother gets her hands on you and you don't get a chance to breathe."

"Is she upset that I slept so long?" I asked, taking a seat across from Grandmother.

"I wouldn't say she's upset. Livid, yes, upset, no. I understand she almost beat your door down trying to wake you. That must have been some spell you used to keep her out. Be prepared for a royal scolding," she said, smiling at her own joke. "She wanted you for more fittings for your gown, but I'm sure she's made do just fine."

A page ran past carrying a basket of flowers. Three others stood on ladders while hanging garlands over doorways. Grassina and Haywood presided over them all from the center of the Hall.

"I thought I should tell you before you heard it from someone else," said Grandmother. "We already had our first fairy-related near-disaster. But don't worry, I took care of it."

"What happened?" I asked with a sick feeling in my stomach.

We waited while a serving maid approached the table and set a mug of cider in front of Grandmother. She smiled at both of us and left to get one for me.

Grandmother looked around as if to make sure that we weren't about to be interrupted again, then said, "Sir Geoffrey, a very sweet and well-intentioned knight, was returning from patrol when he dismounted to pick a wildflower for Lady Eleanor, one of Frazzela's ladies-in-waiting. Unfortunately, a flower fairy on her way to the wedding had stopped for a sip of nectar and was inside the partially closed flower when he snapped the stem. Sir Geoffrey had almost reached the gate when the furious fairy turned him into a chipmunk. A guard who saw the knight disappear into his clothes came looking for me. I was the logical choice since I'd already let everyone know that I'm a witch."

"You didn't!" I said.

"Of course I did. I'm not ashamed of who I am. All this tiptoeing around the subject gives me a headache. If these people have a problem with magic, it's their problem, not mine. As I was saying," she said, giving me a pointed look, "I calmed the fairy and got her to reverse her magic. She was very understanding once I explained it all to her. Fairies believe in true love just like you and me. There was one condition, however."

"And what was that?" I asked, fearing the worst.

Grandmother smiled. "They have to get married and invite her to their wedding, that's all. Neither of them minded in the least."

"Was that the fairy's condition or yours?"

Grandmother's smile got bigger. "Does it matter? Either way, they're getting married next month and I'm invited, too."

I smiled at the serving maid who gave me my cider, then said to Grandmother as the girl walked away, "What happened when you told everyone that you're a witch? How did they take the news?"

"They were a little standoffish until I said a spell to fix the broken pots in the kitchen and another to rebuild a crumbling section of that causeway they're all so worried about. They became quite friendly after that."

"I didn't know they were having any problems," I said.

Grandmother peered at me over her mug of cider. "Everyone has problems. You just have to keep your ears open and help where you can."

"How is Queen Frazzela today? Is she still upset because we invited the fairies?"

"Not at all. She was quite taken with them after she saw one this morning. Listen, I think I hear more arriving now."

She was right. When I tuned out the voices of the people in the Hall, I could hear a faint sound like wind chimes. The sound grew louder as I ran to the courtyard, wanting to make sure that someone was ready to greet them. Queen Frazzela was there already, so caught up in the fairies' arrival that she didn't notice me.

Unlike the flower fairy, these fairies were as big as humans, although finer boned and with more delicate features. The queen seemed captivated by their sweet voices and the graceful way they moved. She smiled and was gracious to them, just the opposite of the way she'd treated me. I even heard her claim that she had insisted that we invite them and that she was so glad they had come.

Bradston was there, too, of course, and was as curious about them as any ten-year-old would have been. I saw him surreptitiously touch the wing of one of the fairies, and held my breath when the fairy turned around, startled. Seeing the boy, her face relaxed in a gentle smile and I knew that what I'd heard was true: fairies were more tolerant of children than they were of adults.

I was going back into the castle when my mother finally found me. "There you are!" she said. "I hate it when you lock your door that way. I can never get in to see you when I have something important to discuss. You knew you had more fittings to do. Why did you sleep so late? Frazzela got Eadric up at dawn and he's been busy ever since."

"We can go see about those fittings now if you'd like," I said, not wanting to argue with her.

"It's too late for that," she said. "Maude had to work with what she had. That gown had better fit, that's all I have to say. It will be your own fault if you look gawky. Three seamstresses working together might have been able to disguise some of your flaws, but even they can't work miracles without fittings."

"I can always use magic to make it fit," I said, then bit my lip when I remembered who I was talking to.

My mother glared at me. "If I'd wanted my daughter

215

to wear a dress made with magic, I wouldn't have had Maude and the others stay up all night to work on it. You will wear it as it is and be thankful that I went to so much trouble."

"Yes, of course, Mother," I said, feeling sorry for Maude.

"Go to your room and wait for us," Mother ordered. "I'll send a serving girl to tell Maude to meet us there with your gown. And for goodness' sake, don't lock your door!"

Although I would have loved to go to the Great Hall to watch the guests arrive, I knew better than to cross my mother again, so I hurried up to my room. I was just shutting the door behind me when Li'l appeared at my window. Flying to the tapestry on the wall, she latched on with her claws and hung upside down to talk to me. "You'll never guess who I saw in the courtyard! The witches from the Old Witches' Retirement Community!"

"I know," I said. "They arrived yesterday."

"No, not them," said the little bat. "I meant the rest of the witches. Your grandmother didn't invite a few of her friends. She invited all of them!"

I sighed and started to take my hair out of its customary braid. "Poor Frazzela. She won't like that one bit."

There was a knock on my door, and before I could answer, my mother rushed into the room. "Good, you're here. Maude will be along in a moment. She has your gown and Lucy is going to do your hair. You've never been any good at doing it yourself. I don't think you even know how to brush it," she said, poking at a lock of my hair as if it were some loathsome creature she didn't want to touch. "Thank goodness I'm here to see that you look decent for your wedding."

I glanced out the window at the tinkling sound of wind chimes and saw a brightly colored flock fly by. At first glance I thought they were birds or butterflies; then I realized that a large contingent of fairies had arrived. I saw them again as they circled the castle to appreciative applause from the courtyard below. A few minutes after they landed, Grassina came to the door.

"Did you see them?" she asked, out of breath from running. "The fairies from Greater Greensward are here. They all came together, which is amazing in itself. I think this is the first time in years they've done anything as a group. You know they consider this a special event when you see the swamp fairy wearing a new dress of green leaves."

There was another knock on the door, and Maude and Hortense came in carrying my gown and slippers. Maude couldn't stop yawning as she laid the gown on my bed. Lucy squeezed in past them, looking horrified when she saw the size of my room. "I'd better go," said Grassina. "You need the space. Call me if I can help in any way."

My grandmother was the next to arrive. When she saw how many people were already there, she pushed past them and took a seat on the bed. Hortense was helping me into my gown when Queen Frazzela came to the door. Once again, my mother wouldn't let her in because Bradston was with her. "But I have to talk to Emma," said Queen Frazzela. "The guards have cornered a dragon in the courtyard. Eadric saw them and interceded before they could dispatch the beast. He says the dragon should have received an invitation, but the beast didn't know about the wedding until the fairies told him. Can you imagine? Eadric actually insists that the creature attend the ceremony! I can't understand what's gotten into that boy. Before he met Emma he would have killed it himself. I nearly fainted when I saw it, and he wants to put it in the buttery until the ceremony begins."

"Is it a very big dragon?" I called through the door.

"No, it's quite small as dragons go," Queen Frazzela called back. "But what possible difference could that make?"

"Quite a bit, actually. A large dragon would never fit in the buttery."

"You don't understand," said the queen. "We can't have dragons in the castle! I've come to ask you to talk some sense into him."

"Who, Eadric or Ralf?" I asked. "I agree that Ralf shouldn't have come by himself. He's too young to travel this far without his parents. I think Eadric was right, though. Ralf will be fine in the buttery."

"You'll have to excuse us now," my mother told Queen Frazzela. "The ceremony will begin soon and Emma isn't nearly ready." I smiled when she shut the door firmly in the spluttering queen's face.

My gown was everything a bride could want. It was made of a finely woven cream-colored fabric that hugged my hips and fell to my feet in soft folds. The three seamstresses had embroidered the hem and cuffs with gold and green threads, using designs of vines and flowers. My mother had given me a heavy gold chain to wear low on my hips and a more delicate one to wear around my neck. Lucy took great pride in dressing my hair, brushing it until it glowed and looping a third and even finer gold chain through it. My mother then produced a gold circlet that she set on my head. It was the closest thing I'd ever had to a crown, but far lighter than what my parents wore for formal events. When they had finished, I felt beautiful and everyone assured me that I was.

We waited until Grassina brought me a lush bouquet of roses, lilacs, and lilies, then my mother led the way down the stairs to the Great Hall. The fairies caught my eye right away. Wearing their best and brightest clothes, they would have been dazzling if the sun hadn't already started to set and the Hall hadn't been lit with torches. I saw flower fairies lined up on the window ledges tickling each other and giggling. The ones sitting on the garlands were harder to see because their flower-petal skirts blended in with the brightly colored blossoms. Most of the larger fairies were gathered together at the sides of the Hall as if so many humans made them uncomfortable, although I did see a few scattered fairies seated among the other guests. One fairy was dressed all in moonbeams that made her seem less real than the fairies around her. Another wore a trailing gown of willow leaves that shivered when she moved. The gown of a third was made of violets, the blossoms having been sewn together so carefully that they remained unblemished.

I was ready when my father took my arm to walk me the length of the room. I could hear people murmuring and the priest clearing his throat, but the loudest sound was that of my own heart. Glancing from side to side, I looked to see who was there, my smile frozen in place. I saw Haywood and Grassina gazing at each other with love in their eyes. Hortense was already crying, as was Oculura, who dabbed at her eyes, then took them out and replaced them with fresh ones. Dyspepsia was muttering to her sister about the lateness of the wedding, how she didn't like going home in the dark and how itchy her new gown felt. King Bodamin smiled warmly at me, oblivious to his wife, who stood beside him trying to take a straw away from Bradston. The boy was using the straw to poke the bubbles that covered the gown of the fairy next to him. My grandmother looked wistful and my mother looked distracted, as if she were thinking of a hundred things about my wedding that she wished she had done differently.

And then I looked straight ahead and saw Eadric, and suddenly I didn't have eyes for anything else. He was standing beside the much shorter priest and looked so handsome that I felt my heart skip a beat. His cream-colored tunic and hose had been embroidered in gold and green to match my gown, and a gold circlet identical to mine held his brown curls back from his forehead. But even if he hadn't been dressed in such finery, he would have been the handsomest man there.

When I finally stood beside Eadric, I began to feel shaky and a little light-headed. Eadric must have seen something in the way I looked, because he took my hand and squeezed it. His hand felt warm in mine, and was as reassuring as always.

The priest was young and nervous. He started with a speech that sounded memorized, saying that although love wasn't essential, it was an important building block in the foundation of a good marriage. Eadric squeezed my hand when the priest paused. We turned to see what he was looking at and saw Li'l and Garrid nestled in the shadow of a banner.

The priest started over, then got as far as the next building block, loyalty, before losing his place again. A minor scuffle had broken out when one of the guards had stepped on Ralf's tail. It seemed to take forever before the priest reached the third element, friendship.

Eadric squeezed my hand once more and I returned

the pressure, knowing that all three building blocks were already ours. The priest hadn't said anything that we didn't already know. Eadric must have thought so, too, because he winked at me and grinned. After that I missed half of what the priest said because I was looking into Eadric's eyes and remembering how they had looked on the day we met. He had been a frog and I'd thought he was obnoxious. Back then I never would have imagined that I would marry him, or that I could love anyone so much.

The priest droned on, interjecting the appropriate questions here and there. I suppose I must have said what I needed to, because before I knew it he was saying, "I now pronounce you man and wife. You may kiss the bride," and Eadric was. It was a long kiss, a warm and sweet kiss full of shared memories and the promise of things to come. It would have lasted even longer if a soldier hadn't clattered into the hall and barged past the assembled guests to King Bodamin's side.

Although the soldier spoke in a lowered tone, I heard everything he said. "We have a situation, Your Majesty. A patrol has sighted trolls carrying clubs coming this way in great numbers. Should we raise the drawbridge?"

"By all means!" exclaimed King Bodamin. "Hurry, man, go give the order."

Apparently I wasn't the only one to hear him, because the fairies and some of the witches began repeating what the soldier had said. He had already gone, but as word spread, knights began to hurry from the Hall as well.

Of the people who remained, the fairies seemed the most agitated. Eadric and I were still standing in front of the priest when one of the fairies from Upper Montevista fluttered her wings and flew over the heads of the other guests to join us. "We apologize, Your Highnesses, but we must go," she said. "We are grateful that you invited us to help celebrate your wedding. However, we believe that the trolls are about to attack this castle. As we must preserve our neutrality in such matters, we think it best that we leave before any fighting begins."

"You're leaving?" Eadric said, sounding incredulous.

The fairy nodded. "Unfortunately. We'll return when the battle is over, provided that the castle is still here. Congratulations on your wedding. It was a lovely ceremony." The fairy raised her hand as a signal to the rest. Within a minute, there wasn't a fairy left in the castle.

"I can't believe it," said Queen Frazzela. "That was the rudest behavior I've ever seen! They accept our gracious invitation, enjoy our hospitality, then can't be bothered to help us when we most need it. I knew all along that we shouldn't have invited them!"

Bradston tugged on her sleeve. "But you said . . ."

"Never mind," the queen snapped, looking doubly annoyed. "Some things do not bear repeating."

Fifteen

The approach of the trolls made it impossible for anyone to leave by conventional means, which meant that everyone not charged with defending the castle had to gather in the Great Hall or other rooms of the keep, the most defensible area. As it was dark out, Eadric and I collected torches to carry up to the battlements to learn what we could. Ralf wanted to accompany us, but we convinced him that he could help more by staying behind to protect the women and children. He decided that this meant watching over Bradston and his mother, so he plopped down in front of them and growled when anyone came near. Queen Frazzela nearly fainted the first time he did this, although Bradston seemed delighted with the little dragon.

When they saw us going, Grassina, Haywood, and my grandmother followed us to the courtyard and up the steps to the battlements, where my father and King Bodamin were already watching the trolls. Neither of them

224

seemed too worried at first. "They can't do anything from there," said Bodamin as the trolls jumped up and down and shouted at us from the far side of the gap separating the ridge from Castle Peak.

While the trolls milled around, lighting torches and bumping into each other, a few of the old witches from the retirement community joined us. The witches were trying to guess what the trolls would do next when the troll queen strode down the middle of the ridge, pushing aside anyone who got in her way. Although she was shorter than most of them, she had more heads than any of the rest. Even the bigger trolls seemed to be afraid of her. When she reached the point on the ridge where the drawbridge would have landed had we set it down, she stopped and shouted with all four heads at once, "King Bodamin!" The volume was impressive, even from so far away.

"That's the troll queen," I told him. "I think the second head from the right is in charge. Its name is Fatlippia."

"What kind of a name is that?" said the king. Cupping his hands around his mouth, he shouted back, "What do you want? Why are you here?"

"We want prince!" shouted Fatlippia.

King Bodamin's eyes went hard and his hands squeezed into fists. "Never!" he shouted. Turning his back on the queen, he told us, "She's not getting Bradston back, even if she lays siege to this castle for a hundred years!"

"Then we come get him!" screamed the head called Ingabinga. "That prince ours! He promise marry queen!" The troll queen turned and was storming away when the strawberry-blonde head called Tizzy looked over her shoulder and stuck out her tongue.

"Marry!" said King Bodamin. "I can't believe Bradston would promise to marry her."

"I don't think he did," said Eadric.

A new troll had arrived and was barking orders, arranging the troll army in a raggedy line. He had two heads like the one who had seemed to be in charge during their attack near the stream—the one who had held the magic-seeing ball. We were wondering what he had planned when he shouted something at the first troll in the line, gesturing from him to us. The troll balked at what must have been an order. When he didn't move, the commanding troll shouted at the second troll. The two trolls squabbled, then the second shoved the first over the edge of the causeway.

The commanding troll barked his order again. Now that the second troll was at the head of the line, he didn't seem to like the order any better than the first had. Instead of waiting for the troll behind to push him, however, he shouted at his commander, then jumped as far as he could with his arms flailing as if they could carry him all the way to where we stood. They didn't, of course, and we watched as he passed out of sight, wailing the whole way down.

"What are they thinking?" my father said as the trolls continued to line up and jump. None of the trolls was getting anywhere near us, yet that didn't seem to deter their commanding troll. One by one they leaped and fell wailing onto the rocks below.

"Trolls don't think," said King Bodamin. "Their brains are smaller than ours."

Eadric had been leaning over the edge of the battlement with a torch in his hand, trying to see farther down Castle Peak. "Emma, could you make me some witches' lights?" he asked when the torch wasn't enough. Whatever moon was out that night was hidden behind the mountain looming above us. Aside from a few twinkling stars, the only light was what we provided. After I'd made him a score of lights, he had me send some of the glowing balls down into the ravine separating Castle Peak from the ridge. Peering over the edge again, he grunted and stepped back. "Look down there," he said, pointing. "Their brains may be smaller, but some of them can think just fine."

From where we stood on the battlement, if we craned our necks just right and leaned out just so, we could see where some of the trolls had landed. Instead of splatting on the rocks, they had grabbed hold and were climbing hand over hand.

"Does anyone know how they're doing that?" asked my father.

When no one could answer him, Grassina took out

her farseeing ball and asked to see one of the climbing trolls. The image in the ball was small, but it was enough to see that the troll was digging his long fingernails into the rock itself, not even bothering to look for crevices.

"Wow," said Eadric. "If their nails are that strong, it's no wonder they're so long. They probably can't even be cut! Look at those trolls go!"

Nearly a dozen trolls had climbed into view, and more appeared as we watched. I glanced at their commander and saw that he was still ordering the trolls over the edge one at a time. Some wailed, but the more resigned ones fell silently.

"I know what to do," said King Bodamin, and he turned to an officer awaiting his orders. They spoke for just a moment, then the officer strode off and the king returned to where we stood. "Now watch," he said. "This should take care of them."

While some soldiers ran down a ramp, others began shooting arrows at the trolls, moving so quickly that the projectiles looked like a swarm of oversized wasps. The arrows bounced off the trolls' backs, although one went straight into the open mouth of a troll who was looking up. He bit down, then smiled, grabbed the next arrow that came near him, and devoured it, too.

Within a few minutes, the first group of soldiers returned, lugging a pot of boiling oil up the ramp. Hauling it to the edge of the parapet, they poured it over the edge onto the trolls below. We could hear the oil splashing on the rocks, but none of the trolls fell, and not one made a sound when the boiling oil drenched them.

"That won't do anything except clean them off and make them smell better," said my grandmother. "Their skin is much thicker than ours, more hide than skin really. It can't be cut, pierced, or burned, unless of course you have a magical ax made specifically to use on trolls." She glanced at King Bodamin. "I don't suppose anyone here has . . ." When he shook his head, Grandmother sighed. "No, I didn't think so. Perhaps we could hold them off until dawn, when daylight will turn them to stone."

King Bodamin snorted.

"I admit that you don't see stone trolls very often," said Grandmother. "Trolls are very conscious of what their fate would be if they didn't get under cover before the sun came up. That's why they attack only at night."

"This has to work," said King Bodamin. His brow was creased and his eyes were hooded when he came back from speaking with his officer a second time. Instead of talking to us, he went to the parapet and leaned over to watch.

The soldiers tried boiling oil again, sending the contents of a dozen enormous pots onto the heads of the trolls. When that didn't work, they tried pot after pot of boiling water. When they ran out of water, they poured dirty water from scrubbing the kitchen floor and the remnants of a cream-based soup that had gone bad the day before but hadn't been thrown out yet. None of this fazed the trolls, who just kept climbing higher.

The king had his men try stones next. The smaller gravel sounded like rushing water when it fell, tumbling over the trolls and clearing off debris. The larger ones bounced against Castle Peak, breaking off chunks. The largest stones knocked a few trolls off the wall, but they just started climbing all over again.

"There must be something you can do," King Bodamin said to Grandmother, Grassina, Haywood, and me. "Some magic that would get rid of them. We know you can turn people into frogs. Can't you turn trolls into something equally harmless?"

"We could try," said Grandmother, "but it wouldn't make any real difference. Our magic doesn't work on trolls the same way it does humans."

King Bodamin's face flushed red. "I know how it is! This isn't your castle, so you don't care what happens to it. You can just fly away on your broomsticks and leave us here to face them when they . . ."

"Oh, all right," said Grandmother, sounding exasperated. "I'll show you what I mean. Do you see that horrid-looking fellow with the big ears? Watch what happens to him."

The troll she was talking about had almost reached the base of the castle itself. He was reaching for his next fingernail-hold when Grandmother cast a spell to turn him into a mouse. The troll paused for a moment, swatting at the air around his head as if a swarm of flies was bothering him, then continued to climb. We all peered down at him, wondering if anything had happened. As he came closer, we saw that he had changed, but not the way the king had wanted. His ears, usually big and pointed, were now small and rounded. His face had become pointier with a row of tiny teeth, and a long, thin tail sprouted from a hole in the seat of his pants. Unfortunately, he was as big and mean and troll-like as ever.

"All right," said King Bodamin. "You can't change the trolls themselves, but surely you can do something else."

"We could call up a storm," I said. "Although I doubt it would do much."

"A storm . . . Yes, that might work," said the king. "A big, fierce storm that will blow them from here to tomorrow."

"All right," I said, "but everyone who isn't a witch has to go inside. A storm strong enough to blow trolls off the side of a mountain will most certainly be strong enough to blow you away as well."

King Bodamin protested, as did Eadric and my father. I relented and let them stay as long as they tied themselves down, but insisted that the soldiers leave, saying that I wouldn't begin until they did. When everyone was ready, I started the storm by myself; then the other witches joined in, adding their strength to mine. It was impressive, with winds that sent boulders flying like specks of dust and ripped the words from our mouths before we could speak.

The other witches and I used magic to keep us in place, so I was able to look over the edge to see how the storm had affected the trolls. Most of them had stopped climbing. Although the trolls' fingernails were still embedded in the rock, the rest of their bodies were flapping like clean laundry in the wind. Only the trolls who had thought quickly enough to use their toenails as well were making any headway, but slowly because they had to move one foot or hand at a time.

We kept the winds blowing until it was obvious to everyone that it wasn't going to work either. Even King Bodamin admitted that we had to give up, if only so we could try something else. We couldn't think of anything else to try, however. The trolls had almost reached the top of the castle walls when my father ordered us inside. King Bodamin protested, still hoping that we could do something that would rid him of the trolls.

Grassina dragged me to the steps leading down to the courtyard. I was partway down, pushed along by the press of old witches behind us, when I realized that Eadric wasn't there. "Where's Eadric?" I called out. "Has anyone seen him?"

"He's back there," shouted a witch at the end of the

line. "I heard him talking about someone named Birdy."

"You mean Ferdy?" I turned and squeezed past my aunt and the other witches, heading back up the stairs. If Eadric was out there, he must think that his magic sword could work against trolls. "Ferdy doesn't have the right kind of magic!" I shouted, running up the last few steps.

"Shh!" said Eadric's father from where he stood just outside the door. "Let him see what he can do."

"But . . . ," I began.

My father grabbed my arm and pulled me out of the way. "If the man wants to try, why not let him?"

Eadric was facing the meanest-looking, ugliest troll I'd ever seen. He was hunchbacked, knock-kneed, and had a nose like a potato. He also had tiny, rounded ears and sharp little teeth that . . . It was the troll that Grandmother had tried to change into a mouse.

The troll hopped off the parapet, landing with a *thunk!* He didn't seem to notice that he had grown a long, thin tail until it snagged in a crack in the parapet. Eadric was already pulling Ferdy from his scabbard when the troll grunted and stopped to look behind him. Seeing his tail, he grabbed it and yanked, howling when it hurt. He forgot his tail, however, when Ferdy began to sing.

> A troll, a troll, I've never fought a troll
> Though there's been many times that I've
>   wanted to.

> To fight a troll—that has become my goal.
> I'll take a couple whacks, then I'll run him
>   through.

The troll roared, opening his mouth so wide that we could see his tiny teeth and his huge gullet. Ferdy didn't wait for him to finish. He whacked the troll, just as he said he would—one, two, three! Neat slits appeared in the troll's ragged clothes, but his hairy hide was unharmed underneath. However, Ferdy wasn't about to give up.

> This troll is tough, his skin so thick—
> Defeating him won't be so quick.
> Give me just a minute more
> And he'll be laid out on the floor!

The troll lumbered as far as his still-caught tail would let him while Ferdy whacked away until the raggedy clothes hung in ribbons. When the troll reached for Ferdy, the sword jumped aside, then whacked the creature's hands like a teacher slapping a wayward student.

The troll growled, unhurt but obviously angry. "Hold still!" he bellowed. "Me get you!"

Instead of going for Ferdy again as I thought he would, the troll buffeted the sword aside and reached for Eadric, wrapping his beefy hands around his neck. I shrieked, then bit my lip and thought furiously, knowing that with a twitch of his fingers the troll could snap Eadric's neck in an instant. Because trolls seemed to be constantly hungry, I thought a little distraction might help. The troll's mousy tendencies gave me an idea for the spell.

Stop that troll, if you please.
Hit him with a wheel of cheese!

A huge wheel of yellow cheese shot out of nowhere, thumping the troll soundly in the chest. He looked surprised, then delighted when he saw the cheese spinning on the floor where it had landed. "Yummy!" he bellowed. Letting go of Eadric, the troll lunged after the cheese, jerking to a stop when he reached the length of his tail.

While the troll struggled to free himself, I ran to Eadric and grabbed him by the back of his tunic. "Come on," I said, trying to pull him toward the steps.

Coughing and rubbing his throat, Eadric turned and followed me. Our fathers were already halfway down when we reached the stairs. Hearing another troll land on the floor lent us speed, and we dashed down to the courtyard, nearly stepping on the kings' heels.

One after the other the trolls crawled over the parapet. As we crossed the courtyard, heading for the keep, the first trolls started down the steps behind us. Haywood was waiting for us, and the moment we crossed the threshold, he said a spell that made the door as immovable as the stone walls around it. Now nothing could open that door until he undid the spell. We were discussing what we should do next when we heard something heavy crash against the door, but it was stronger now than its original wood, and the trolls couldn't even make it rattle.

"What about the other doors?" asked my father.

"The witches from the retirement community are taking care of those," said Haywood.

"The trolls are climbing the walls of the keep!" Grassina shouted from the entrance to the Great Hall.

"They must be going for the windows," said Haywood. "We'll have to take care of those next."

The arrow slits were too narrow for a troll to fit through, but the windows facing the valley were wide enough. When Grandmother's friends had finished with the doors, they went from window to window, shrinking them so that even a troll's hand wouldn't have fit. Although the rest of the castle might be overrun with trolls, the keep would be impenetrable once every door and window was blocked.

As soon as the witches were finished, we met in the Great Hall to try to come up with some way of evicting the trolls. "We're safe enough here," said King Bodamin. "I have soldiers stationed around the keep, watching the trolls through the arrow slits. They'll keep us posted if the trolls try anything new."

"We're trapped, aren't we?" said my mother.

King Bodamin's expression was fierce. "Only magic could get us out now."

"Has anyone seen the troll queen?" I asked. When no one could answer me, I took out my farseeing ball and asked to see her. At first I couldn't figure out where she was. She was using her nails to climb up a small, narrow space. Her four heads made hideous faces as they squeezed through the opening and she climbed out into . . .

"That's the garderobe down the hall from my room!" Bradston shouted into my ear. I hadn't known that he was peering over my shoulder, so I jumped when he shouted, and the image in the ball disappeared. I knew the garderobe he was talking about, however. It was a tiny room that jutted out from the side of the castle like a wart on a troll's nose. The hole of the garderobe emptied into the valley, making an easy entrance for anyone who climbed the wall on that side, provided they weren't too squeamish.

"She's in the castle?" said Queen Frazzela, her voice high and shrill.

Bradston pointed overhead. "She's . . ."

Then we all heard her, whooping and yelling as she thundered through the corridor *above* the Great Hall, growing louder as she drew closer. Queen Frazzela became so pale that I was sure she was about to faint. "Can't someone do something?" she whispered.

The troll queen tore down the steps, her four heads

screaming. Each was wild-eyed and covered with filth. A row of soldiers stood ready to defend us, forcing us to peer around them to see the queen. The closer she came, the better we could see her faces, lumpy with dried scabs left by the troll pox, and colored with garish paint that highlighted her eyes and mouths.

The troll queen fought the soldiers, their swords and pikes bouncing off her as she beat them back with the cudgels she held in her hands. She was almost through the line when Eadric tried to pull me behind him, but I stood my ground and said a spell that would have stopped most people. I didn't know if it would hurt her, but then I didn't know if anything could.

> Let the ground beneath her open
> To a deep and noisome pit.
> Put inside it snakes with venom
> Of the kind that bite or spit.

One moment the troll queen was coming after me, the next the ground had opened under her and she'd disappeared. I cringed, wondering if I'd gone too far. I'd never intentionally hurt anyone before, and the thought that I had made me feel cold inside. Everyone froze, listening for some sound from the pit, afraid that they might actually hear it. After a dreadful silence the witches began arguing about who should retrieve her body. My father suggested that I seal her in, but King Bodamin didn't want me to, saying that if the troll queen was still alive down there, she might find some way to undermine the castle foundations and kill everyone.

While the two kings debated what to do, the witches prepared to draw straws to see who would go into the hole. I was watching them when Queen Frazzela shrieked and pointed at the hole. The troll queen's heads had risen over the edge and she was crawling out, dragging herself by her nails.

However frightening she'd looked before, it was nothing compared with how she looked now. Her filthy clothes had been torn when she'd fallen into the snake pit, and what was left of them writhed as if they'd taken on a life of their own. Bulges rippled and slid across her stomach, then over her chest and down her arm. A snake slipped out of a hole in her sleeve, its tongue flicking the air. She grabbed it just behind the head and bit it while the tail thrashed and twitched. After she'd eaten the entire snake, savoring each bite, she used her nails to dig the scales from her teeth.

More soldiers had positioned themselves between the troll queen and the royal family. I'd have to do something before she hurt anyone else, but first I needed some questions answered. "Why do you want the prince?" I said. "Do you honestly want to marry him?"

"Prince promised to me. He mine!" Fatlippia said as the troll queen stopped short.

Queen Frazzela gasped and began to cry.

"Did you promise the troll queen that you'd marry her?" King Bodamin asked his youngest son as he shook him by the shoulder.

Bradston gulped and shook his head. "I didn't promise her anything."

"Then what is she talking about?" asked the king.

"Who promised that you could marry the prince?" I called to the troll queen.

"Two humans," said Tizzy. "Young one and old one. Came through magic mirror. Said if queen took young prince, queen have husband and human kingdom. Humans warn queen about you. Old one say you come if queen took prince. Gave queen two balls show magic. Young one tell where prince hunt eggs."

"What did the humans look like?" Eadric asked, pushing me to the side.

Grunella leaned toward Fatlippia, whispering, "That prince I tell about."

After studying Eadric a moment, Fatlippia nodded and whispered back, "I see what Grunella mean." Raising her voice, she told him, "Young one hair color of straw and eyes like summer sky. Old one no hair on top and big belly."

Eadric glanced at me. "Sounds like Jorge and Olebald."

"They had no right to promise you the prince," I told her. "Bradston can't go with you."

Curling her lip, Fatlippia shook her head. "Queen not want that one. He talk too much. Queen want that one," she said, pointing at Eadric. "Grunella say he prince, too."

Eadric grunted as if he'd been hit in the stomach. "You can't have him either," I said. "I just married him. He's mine now."

I could have sworn I heard Fatlippia growl. The other heads looked at her as if they were expecting something to happen. "No human tell queen what can and can't do," she said, narrowing her eyes. Raising her clubs to shoulder height, she began to twirl them like a child might twirl a length of rope. The clubs went faster and faster, making an awful whining shriek that hurt my ears. When the troll queen reached the soldiers, her clubs were an unstoppable force that cut them down like grain before a scythe. After finishing with the soldiers, the troll queen turned her eyes on me.

"Kill her, Fatlippia! If she dead, prince not belong to anyone," called the head named Grunella.

Everyone except Eadric and I had fled to the back of the Hall. Unlike my family's castle, however, there were no doors there to allow them to escape. The only thing behind the Great Hall in Upper Montevista was the valley and a thousand-foot drop. "Get back!" Eadric shouted at me, pulling Ferdy from his scabbard.

"A troll, a troll . . . ," the singing sword began.

"No," I told him. "You heard the queen. This fight is

mine!" And then I did something I'd never intended to do in front of my new husband's family again. The first time I'd done it, it had made them hate me and could have ended any chance I had of marrying my one true love. Now I didn't see that I had any choice if I was to save him from the troll. Closing my eyes, I said the same spell that I'd used at the tournament and many times since.

The shriek was torn from my throat as my body began to burn. I felt as though the spell was peeling off my skin and replacing my bones with lava. It was excruciating, but when it ended abruptly, I stood before the troll queen a peridot green dragon, more than twice as long as she was tall, ready to defend all the humans in the room.

"Look!" said Ingabinga.

"Maybe we go home now," said Grunella.

"I not quitter!" growled Fatlippia. "That prince mine!" Roaring her rage, she launched herself at me, her clubs moving so fast that they were hard to see.

I reared up, glad that I'd eaten gunga beans and hot flami-peppers only the week before. As the troll queen twirled her clubs, I took a deep breath and exhaled, igniting her clothes, her hair, and the banners hanging on the walls behind her. The witches in the Hall doused the flames and wafted the smoke out the window while the troll queen began to pound me with her cudgels. I beat my wings once and rose above her now-hairless heads.

Although the troll queen was strong, I knew that I was

stronger. With the witches waiting to undo any damage I might accidentally inflict on the castle, I whipped around and hit her with my tail, knocking her through the tables and benches so that she hit the far wall with a crash.

The queen staggered to her feet and shook her heads, then came after me with a roar. Hitting me with both clubs at the same time, she sent me spinning upward so that I slammed into the ceiling. The beams cracked; the ceiling disintegrated. The witches caught the debris before it could hit anyone while I snagged the troll queen with my claws. I tried to bite her, but she rammed her hand into my mouth and tried to pull out my tongue. I shook her like a dog does a rat, so she hit me over the head with her clubs. When I opened my jaws and dropped her onto the floor, she sat up, cursing.

I landed beside her, my sides heaving as I gasped for air. "You can't have him," I said when I had the breath to speak.

The troll queen's breathing was ragged when she wiped the ashes of her singed-off hair from her unscathed scalp. "I not take him now, but I not give up. I come back later when you not look."

"Are you sure you want him?" I asked.

Trying to turn Eadric into a dragon would surely kill him, but there was something that I could do that might work just as well. While the queen pushed herself off the floor, I thought of the magic that Olebald Wizard had used in the battle against my father's army. His dragons had been illusions, complete except for their lack of a dragony smell. I could use something like it, but only if the troll queen wasn't as observant as I had been.

"*Psst,* Eadric," I whispered. "Just play along."

"What are you planning?" he asked.

"You'll understand in a minute," I said, and I whispered the spell that seemed to transform Eadric.

The dragon appeared so suddenly that all four of the troll queen's heads gasped. He was an orange dragon, just as Olebald's had been. And just like Olebald's pretend dragons, he was huge. When he reared back, his head nearly touched the ceiling. Even though I had made the magic and knew that he wasn't real, I was impressed.

"Go home," said Eadric, although it sounded as if the dragon were speaking. "I'll never marry you. If you try to take me back to your cave, I'll become my true self and eat you alive."

Fatlippia and Grunella leaned toward each other until their foreheads touched. They began to whisper, but I could still hear what they said.

"This worse than first prince," said Grunella.

"First prince may be dragon, too," Fatlippia said. "Maybe whole family is."

Grunella shuddered. "I not want dragon husband. Cannot tell what to do."

"Then why marry human?" said Fatlippia. When she sighed, she actually sounded sad. "Maybe marriage not for us. Being spinster not so bad. Still have one another."

The last sound I heard as the troll queen stomped from the Great Hall was the mournful wailing of the other three heads.

Sixteen

*I*f the troll queen hadn't been so awful, I might have felt sorry enough for her to help her find someone else, but she was mean and nasty, and I wouldn't want to inflict her on anyone I knew, unless . . . The most wonderful idea popped into my head, and the more I thought about it, the more I liked it. The queen wanted a prince for a husband, and I knew the perfect man for her. He would be just what she wanted, and she would be just what he deserved.

The troll queen was about to try bashing down the door with her clubs when I found her. Rather than have another door to fix, I asked Haywood to remove his spell. Everyone else stayed behind while I followed the troll queen outside.

"What you want?" she snapped at me as her trolls assembled behind her. I was still a dragon, so they were careful to keep their distance.

I made myself comfortable on the paving stones and

wrapped my tail around me. "Just because you can't marry Eadric or Bradston doesn't mean that you can't marry anyone," I said. "I happen to know an available prince who would be just right for you. You've already met him. It's that young man, Jorge, who came to see you through a magic mirror. Do you think he would do?"

Grunella's eyes lit up while Ingabinga and Tizzy began talking at once. "He do fine!" said Tizzy. "How we find him?" asked Ingabinga. "We not know where he live."

"But I do," I replied.

"I not sure this idea good," said Fatlippia.

Tizzy stuck out her lower lip. "It not fair. We always do what Fatlippia want."

Grunella nodded. "We going even if Fatlippia not like!"

Fatlippia seemed surprised by their vehemence. "If that what three heads really want . . . ," she said.

The other heads cheered. Following their lead, the troll army shouted and stomped their feet even though they had no idea what was going on. When the ruckus died down, Fatlippia turned to me and said, "Where you say prince live?"

"I'll tell you, but first I want the other ball like the one I broke," I said.

"I not tell . . . ," began Fatlippia, but I wasn't looking at her. Tizzy's eyes had darted to the commanding troll standing in front of the troll queen. He shoved one of his hands behind his back, but not before I saw the reflection of something shiny.

"Let me see that," I said, uncurling my tail and getting to my feet. When the troll looked like he was about to turn and bolt, I stretched my neck and grabbed him by his leather tunic, then shook him until he dropped the ball. The troll queen dove for it, but I was there first, stepping on it with a loud *crack!*

"Look for the prince in East Aridia," I said, using my claws to scrape the shattered ball into a pile. "Go over the mountains and cross the River Sludge. His castle is in the city of Raveen."

Fatlippia scowled at me, but it was Grunella who said, "We go now. It time troll queen have husband!"

❧

I remained a dragon until the last of the trolls had crossed the drawbridge and were well on their way to East Aridia. Repairs to the castle had already begun when Eadric found me in the courtyard, a human once again. Hand in hand, we retreated to the sheltered base of an undamaged tower to steal a few moments alone.

"When was the last time I told you that I love you?" I asked after I'd kissed him quite thoroughly.

"At least a few hours ago. I must warn you that my parents can't wait to thank you for getting rid of the trolls, but I'm going to keep you to myself a while longer."

"That sounds good to me," I said, leaning into another kiss.

"You know," Eadric said eventually. "I think my father likes you. He can't stop saying nice things about 'that wonderful Emma.'"

"And what about your mother?"

"I think she's getting tired of Bradston and his tricks. I actually heard her say, 'I've had just about enough of you, young man.'"

"Is that so?" I said. "Tell me, when is your mother's birthday?"

"In a few months. Why?"

"Because if she can manage to be nice to us from now until then, I just might have the perfect gift for her. What do you think she'd say if I ended the spell and gave her some time to herself?"

"I'd say that she'd be mad if she found out that you cast it in the first place."

"And if I told her that if she wasn't nice, I'd do it all over again?"

"Then I think you'd have the nicest mother-in-law in the world."

"Mmm," I murmured as he kissed me again. "That would be perfect. I already have the very best husband in the world."

"And you, my love, are the most unpredictable wife!"

The tinkle of wind chimes announcing the return of

our fairy guests made us both look up. Our chance to be alone was going to be shorter than either of us had hoped.

I sighed and brushed an errant dragon scale from Eadric's tunic. "Someday when we have lots of time, remind me to tell you what you mean to me."

Eadric tilted my head back so he could gaze into my eyes. "I can tell you what you mean to me with just one word."

"Let me guess," I said, smiling up at him. "Maybe I make you happy because you no longer have to enter kissing contests to find the best kisser? Do I bring excitement into your life because I can whisk you away to exotic lands on my magic carpet? Or do you find me delightful because I can conjure food whenever you're hungry?"

"No, that's not . . . Wait, what was that last one?"

I laughed and shook my head. "Never mind. So tell me in one word, what *do* I mean to you?"

"That's easy," said Eadric. "Everything!"